THE PECULIAR NIGHT OF THE BLUE HEART

New York Times bestselling author
Lauren DeStefano

BLOOMSBURY

Praise for Lauren DeStefano

THE PECULIAR NIGHT OF THE BLUE HEART

★ "The story's sure pace, complex characters, creepy moments, and haunting central story of a nearby family's farmyard secret are tender enough to draw in readers who like an emotional story of growth, as well as those who love to experience chills." —*Booklist*, starred review

"Themes of belonging, loss, and what it means to be human underscore the tight storytelling and add depth. . . . Touching and creepy." —*School Library Journal*

"A moving story about the lengths children will go to help a friend. . . . DeStefano again explores the spirit world in an engaging and sometimes frightening way." —*Publishers Weekly*

"Spooky yet heartfelt." —*School Library Connection*

A CURIOUS TALE OF THE IN-BETWEEN

"Young readers will be forgiven if their blood runs cold at certain points of Lauren DeStefano's elegant, disquieting novel." —*The Wall Street Journal*

"Thematically haunting and skillfully executed, this blend of ghost story, family drama, and mystery will leave readers pondering the space between the living and the spirit world for some time." —*BCCB*

"Readers will be hooked from the first line. . . . Love, loss, and hope are at the heart of this exciting read." —*Kirkus Reviews*

"DeStefano creates a beguiling world through haunting images and descriptions. . . . An eerie, moving story." —*Publishers Weekly*

Books by Lauren DeStefano

A Curious Tale of the In-Between
The Peculiar Night of the Blue Heart
The Girl with the Ghost Machine

The Peculiar Night of the Blue Heart

Lauren DeStefano

BLOOMSBURY

NEW YORK   LONDON   OXFORD   NEW DELHI   SYDNEY

First published in the United States of America in September 2016
by Bloomsbury Children's Books
Paperback edition published in June 2017
www.bloomsbury.com

Bloomsbury is a registered trademark of Bloomsbury Publishing Plc

For information about permission to reproduce selections from this book, write to
Permissions, Bloomsbury Children's Books, 1385 Broadway, New York, New York 10018
Bloomsbury books may be purchased for business or promotional use. For information on bulk
purchases please contact Macmillan Corporate and Premium Sales Department at
specialmarkets@macmillan.com

The Library of Congress has cataloged the hardcover edition as follows:
Names: DeStefano, Lauren, author.
Title: The peculiar night of the blue heart / by Lauren DeStefano.
Description: New York : Bloomsbury, 2016
Summary: Lionel, a wild boy, and Marybeth, a good girl, are best friends at the orphanage,
and when a mysterious spirit possesses Marybeth they will do anything to stop it.
Identifiers: LCCN 2015046636 (print) | LCCN 2016021090 (e-book)
ISBN 978-1-61963-643-9 (hardcover) • ISBN 978-1-61963-644-6 (e-book)
Subjects: | CYAC: Best friends—Fiction. | Friendship—Fiction. | Spirit possession—Fiction. |
Orphans—Fiction. | BISAC: JUVENILE FICTION / Fantasy & Magic. | JUVENILE
FICTION / Social Issues / Death & Dying. | JUVENILE FICTION / Family / Parents.
Classification: LCC PZ7.D47 Pdm 2016 (print) | LCC PZ7.D47 (e-book) | DCC [Fic]—dc23
LC record available at https://lccn.loc.gov/2015046636

ISBN 978-1-61963-645-3 (paperback)

Book design by Colleen Andrews and Amanda Bartlett
Typeset by Newgen Knowledge Works (P) Ltd., Chennai, India
Printed and bound in the U.S.A. by Berryville Graphics Inc., Berryville, Virginia
2 4 6 8 10 9 7 5 3 1

All papers used by Bloomsbury Publishing, Inc., are natural, recyclable products
made from wood grown in well-managed forests. The manufacturing processes
conform to the environmental regulations of the country of origin.

For Mary, who is wonderfully peculiar.
Never stop being you.

Childhood is measured out by sounds and smells
And sights, before the dark of reason grows.
—John Betjeman

CHAPTER
1

Lionel was a wild boy. Sometimes he forgot he was a boy at all. He growled and purred, and fell asleep curled beneath the table during breakfast.

Mrs. Mannerd was always exasperated with Lionel, but she had seven other children to mind, and some days it was easier to serve him his porridge under the table than it was to make him use a chair.

Lionel might have been useful if only he'd been cooperative. When he talked to the chickens, they would lay eggs, but he would not dare steal them from the roosts. He was so patient and so still and so endearing that he could lure a wild rabbit into his hands, but he would not allow Mr. Porter, the butcher, to skin it for supper. One afternoon he walked into the barn just as Mr. Porter was about to take an ax to the Thanksgiving turkey, and he screamed and caused such a ruckus that the turkey was spooked and took off running, and feeble old Mr. Porter had to chase it around the barn with his bad back and his ax in one hand, all as Lionel shouted, "Run, run!" and tried to set the turkey free.

It had been a delicious turkey supper, but Lionel spent the whole meal sobbing in the darkness of the stairwell, blowing his nose on the good napkins with the embroidered fleurs-de-lis that the late Ms. Gillingham had imported from France (God rest her soul).

Everyone in the house agreed that the boy was strange, except for Marybeth. Marybeth could often be found following Lionel, and she always offered him some of the pralines that her second cousin sent for the holidays.

Marybeth was a very normal girl, with dark hair that she wore braided into pigtails, and round spectacles with red metal rims. She always washed her face and brushed her teeth without being asked, and what she wanted with a boy like Lionel was perplexing to everyone in the house.

Mrs. Mannerd hoped that some of Marybeth's graces would rub off on the boy. Marybeth was nine and Lionel was nine and three-quarters, but she was at least five years wiser—or so Mrs. Mannerd liked to say.

But Marybeth hoped she wasn't an influence on Lionel; she quite liked him the way he was: clever and brave, as though he could never be harmed simply because it never occurred to him.

Before she followed him outside that morning, Marybeth snuck two of Mrs. Mannerd's coconut cookies into her dress pockets and ran through the screen door in the kitchen. Lionel was already several yards ahead, and she hurried to catch up to him, her braids bouncing against her shoulders. "Where are you going?" she asked him.

It was a question Lionel heard often. He never sat still and he was always going somewhere, and he was always gone for a long time. He was very good at not answering. He would yawn or bite into an apple or howl like a wolf. But he liked Marybeth; she never scolded him or stole his pillow or told him to eat his stew. So he gave her a straight answer. "I'm going to make friends with a fox I saw last week."

"Is it one of Mrs. Rustycoat's babies?" Marybeth asked. Mrs. Rustycoat was the name of a fox they'd found last spring. She wouldn't come close while Marybeth was in tow, but Lionel told her that when he was alone, Mrs. Rustycoat came and ate blueberries from his hand. He said she was so aloof and cautious because she had a litter somewhere.

"It wasn't one of hers," Lionel said. "It had a blue coat."

"Can foxes be blue?" Marybeth asked.

"I've never heard of it," Lionel said. "But I know what I saw. It stood on its hind legs and looked at me and then ran into a shrub."

"Did you look it up in the encyclopedia?" Marybeth asked.

"Mrs. Mannerd says I'm banned from the encyclopedias for a week."

"That's the silliest thing I've ever heard."

"She said they give me wild ideas."

Mrs. Mannerd was an adult, and had been one for a long time. So long, in fact, that the children suspected she had no memory of being a child herself. Her hair was gray and she was very tall. She was afraid of children with wild ideas. She said that she'd been caring for orphans for forty years and she had seen all kinds of children—good ones and mean ones and smart ones and dull ones—but she had never under all her stars had a child like Lionel. She once said that Lionel must have been born in a barn, and Marybeth politely pointed out that Jesus had been born in a barn, and Mrs. Mannerd didn't have anything to say to that except, "Finish your carrots, Marybeth."

Lionel had smiled at her from across the table. Only for a moment, though, and then he dipped his head. He

didn't like for the other children to know what he was thinking.

He was in good spirits now. He stepped into the woods, as light on his feet as a ghost. Marybeth stayed close behind him and tried not to make too much noise. She looked over her shoulder just once, to see how far they'd gone from the little red house where Mrs. Mannerd would be collecting the laundry from the hampers right about now, muttering about things the children left in their pockets. The older ones would be in their rooms studying their French and their cursive, no doubt envious of Marybeth and Lionel, who were the only children young enough to be allowed to squander their Saturday mornings outside.

Not long ago, there had been another child their age, a little girl with long hair and eyes the same color as when the daylight hits the sea. She was extremely polite and curtsied when she said hello. She was adopted by a young couple with kind eyes and creased clothes, and once she was gone, Mrs. Mannerd told the children, "You see what happens when you behave?"

There were infants sometimes as well. They came and went, each one identical to the one before it. Mrs. Mannerd didn't like infants. They always needed something, and they couldn't help out around the house. But they were adopted off soon enough. Babies were preferred by the barren. Best to shape them from the beginning, rather than taking an older child and dealing with who they've already become.

Lionel was certain that nobody would ever adopt him. That suited him just fine. As soon as he was old enough, he would live in the woods and be a wild thing, and he would never eat porridge again.

"Stop," he said, and held out his arms. When the leaves ceased to crunch under Marybeth's scuffed black boots, he listened. The animal was nearby. He could feel its pulse in the air, like the rumble of a train getting closer.

He crouched low, and then he began to crawl.

Marybeth stood still, holding her breath for as long as she could stand just to be quiet.

Finally she said, "It won't come out because I'm here."

Lionel stood. His eyes were distant, and at first Marybeth didn't think he'd heard her, but then he said, "Maybe."

"I can go inside."

"I don't want you to go," Lionel said. He wasn't looking at her, and he gnawed on his lip pensively as he considered the hiding animal, unaware of how his words had touched her. Marybeth, like the other children in the house, was unaccustomed to being told she was wanted.

"Come out, you stubborn thing," Lionel said. "Mr. Porter and the older ones aren't here. It's just us."

"Maybe it's best that it's scared, whatever it is," Marybeth said. "No animal would become supper if it knew to stay away from humans."

"We aren't humans," Lionel said. "We're Lionel and Marybeth."

Sometimes, for just a moment, Marybeth stood on the very edge of his world, and through the shadows she could almost see what he was thinking.

"Come on," she said. "We can go to the river and talk to the fish. They always come to you."

"All right," Lionel said, quite frustrated with the blue creature, who could not, it seemed, know the difference between an ordinary human and Marybeth. He began to suspect he had overestimated the thing's intelligence.

They spent the rest of the morning making faces at the fish and chasing each other, giggling as they caught each other between the trees until Mrs. Mannerd called them to their chores, and they ran to her voice.

That evening, after dinner, Lionel slipped outside as the older ones argued over who got to take the first bath while there was still plenty of hot water.

Mrs. Mannerd knew that Lionel had gone because he'd left the storm door open, and the wind made it flutter against the frame.

She also knew that going after him would prove futile. He was quick as a fox, and he liked to climb. She lost her breath chasing after him, always to no end.

Marybeth, however, was never any trouble to find. She was sitting at the empty table, her posture ever straight as she read from a cover-worn book she'd checked out of the library.

"Do you know where Lionel's gone off to?" Mrs. Mannerd said.

"To feed the foxes, maybe," Marybeth offered. "He had berries in his pocket."

So that was why the blueberries kept disappearing, Mrs. Mannerd thought.

Marybeth closed her book. "I can find him."

"Don't be too long. The sun's going down."

Of all the children in the house, Marybeth was the only one to ever do as she was told, and without complaint, no less. She didn't even need to be reminded to put on her coat before she opened the door.

When Marybeth stepped outside, she was greeted by a gust of cool autumn wind. This was the time of year when Lionel was more prone to disappear. After most of the birds had abandoned their nests in preparation for the winter, he turned his focus to the foxes and rabbits, and left offerings to the coyotes in the hopes of charming them as well.

She knew better than to call out to him. Her voice would only startle whatever small creature he was trying to allure.

She was no expert tracker; she wasn't deft or silent. But she did know Lionel, and she could see the subtle traces that he left on his way out of the house. For starters, he never stepped in the soft earth like the kind that had formed after yesterday's rain. Soft earth left footprints. He would hop over that and tread only in the grass.

Marybeth looked for the grass that was slightly bent. There was an empty patch where she remembered seeing some clovers earlier. They were gone now, which meant that Lionel had plucked them.

He would feed them to the rabbits, she thought. Along with the bits of bark that were missing from a nearby tree.

Moving as quietly as she could, she ascended into the tree line and made her way to the warren.

Sure enough, she found Lionel lying on his stomach, looking into a mossy opening beside a giant tree. He didn't look at Marybeth, but she saw his ears prick up. He was being a rabbit himself just then.

She took a step toward him.

"Quiet," he whispered, and made room for her beside him.

Marybeth lowered herself onto the ground, breathing as quietly as she could.

Lionel looked at her, and only she would have been able to recognize the smile in his eyes, on his face that was otherwise firm with concentration. "There's a fat mother rabbit in there," he said. His voice sounded just like the wind, his words barely audible. "She's shy, but she can't resist the clovers. Give me your hand."

Marybeth held out her hand, watching curiously as he filled her palm with rumpled clovers.

"Hold it up by the entrance," he said, nodding to the small cavern. "Go on."

Marybeth did as he instructed with a sense of caution. Lionel sometimes tried to include her in his endeavors with wild creatures, but she lacked his natural magic. She always ended up scaring the poor things away.

For several seconds, nothing happened. It was beginning to get dark, and soon Mrs. Mannerd would grow cross with them.

"Lionel—"

"Shh. Shh. Look."

Marybeth sensed the rabbit before she saw it. It peeked its gray-brown head from its warren and twitched its nose against her fingertip. Marybeth felt a chill and did her best not to giggle.

Bit by bit, the rabbit came out into view. It really was

a chubby thing, and it went for the clovers in Marybeth's palm. It looked at her with its nervous black eyes as it chewed.

Lionel talked softly to it, murmuring sweet things mothers said to sleeping babies—or so Marybeth would imagine—and stroking its cheek with his knuckle.

A sharp gust of wind pushed across the sky, rattling the bare branches and fallen leaves. The rabbit's ear twitched, and it hopped back into hiding.

Marybeth burst into giggles and rolled onto her side. "I don't think she liked me very much."

"Sure she did," Lionel said. "It's taken all week for me to get her to come out." A smile was beginning to creep onto his serious features. Marybeth plucked a blade of grass from his unruly hair.

She was the only one he would allow to do such a thing. When Mrs. Mannerd attempted to comb his hair, he hissed. *Be reasonable!* Mrs. Mannerd would cry, which of course only made him less reasonable. But Marybeth never told him what to do. She never tried to tame him, not even when she didn't understand why he behaved the way that he did. She merely cared for him, the way that he cared for the rabbits. The way a mother bird guarded her nest.

"What did you do with the berries you took?" she asked.

"I left them by the river. I'm sure I saw the blue fox go there."

Marybeth stared at the bit of clovers still in her palm. It was a simple-enough thing, a clover; people stepped over them on their way to grander things. But she knew that it was the greatest thing Lionel had to offer her. It was an invitation into his peculiar world.

From far away, they heard the storm door open.

"Children!" Mrs. Mannerd called.

Marybeth cringed. "I was supposed to find you and bring you back inside." She stood and held out her hands. He took them, and she pulled him to his feet.

The smile was still lingering on his face, and it grew. "Race you back."

He took off running before she could answer.

"Lionel!"

He held an unfair advantage, and he knew it. He was barefoot while she wore stiff leather shoes that were secondhand and a size too small. And when he had a mind to be, he was the wind itself, flying over the surface of the earth, impossible to catch.

But when he reached the side of the little red house, he waited for her. That was the thing that made him human again.

CHAPTER 2

The wind and rain picked up late that night. The older ones did not notice storms, and they slept on.

Marybeth shared a bedroom with three older girls, and she slept on the rickety top bunk beside the window that overlooked the woods. There was a maple tree that grew beside the house, and its branches would rap on the glass when it was especially windy, as though it wanted to wake her and show her something.

Only there was never anything out there to see. Marybeth rubbed the sleep from her eyes and squinted through the blur of her nearsighted vision.

She was just falling back to sleep when she saw it: a flicker of blue.

She sat upright immediately, unsure if she had dreamed it. She reached for her spectacles, hanging from a nail in the wall above her pillow.

The edges of the swaying trees came into focus. When the branches moved just so, she saw it again, a flash of blue.

She descended the ladder from her bed, minding the missing rung that had broken off before she came to live there.

There were no windows in the upstairs hallway, and without so much as the moonlight to guide her, Marybeth walked with her hand along the wall to make her way.

The door to the boys' room was slightly ajar. Marybeth could hear the older ones snoring.

"Lionel," she whispered. His bed was farthest from the door, in a corner where the ceiling leaked when it rained. He kept a galvanized bucket at the foot of his bed, and Marybeth could hear the *plunk, plunk, plunk* of water falling into it. "Lionel!"

One of the older ones stopped snoring. He sat up, his silhouette all black against a flash of lightning that brightened the window.

"I was dreaming that I was a king, and then you woke me," he told her. "If I'm not still king when I go back to sleep, I'll hang you by your toes."

He might do it, Marybeth knew. She'd been locked

in closets and framed for the older ones' offenses, so that she'd be punished with their chores. The older ones made a game of tormenting Marybeth and Lionel, but Marybeth especially, because she was easier to catch and too timid to defend herself.

"Beat it," the older one said, and Marybeth shrank away from the doorway. If she wanted to look for the blue creature, she would have to go alone and tell Lionel about it in the morning.

She made her way down the stairs, knowing precisely which ones to avoid because they creaked, and took the lantern from the hall closet and struck a match to light the candle. After that, she grabbed her yellow rain slicker from its hook by the door. She wriggled her feet into her rain boots, which were a size too large and beginning to come apart from their soles. They were older than Marybeth herself and had been worn by every child to live in this house before her.

The cold wind filled the house as she opened the door, splattering the floorboards with rain. Marybeth moved quickly, pulling the door shut tight behind her and hoping the sound wouldn't wake Mrs. Mannerd in her bed. She was a light sleeper as it was.

This was not the first time she had snuck out of the house; she had chased after Lionel on his odd adventures, and she had sought sanctuary in the woods so that she might catch up on her reading. But never at night and in such horrible weather. She would have waited until morning if she thought the blue creature would show itself.

She held the lantern ahead of her and tried to see beyond its dull light. She was sure the flash of blue came from along the river, somewhere near the big rock where she and Lionel would lie on their stomachs to watch the fish as he tried to charm them to the surface.

"Are you here?" she said, her soft voice drowned in the wind and rain. No answer. She tried to imitate Lionel's confidence when he spoke to his animals. "Come on out," she said. "There's no one here to hurt you."

If she found this blue light, this fox—or whatever it was—she knew that she would at last understand Lionel the way that she wanted to understand him. For years she had tagged along and tried to be a part of his hidden world, but all she could ever do was watch from the outside.

She stood still for a long time, the rain making its way under her hood and plastering her hair to her neck. Nothing came of it, and her heart sank. The blue creature was gone, if it had ever been there at all. It could have been a dream, or some trick of the light.

She was just about to turn back for the house when she saw it again—a flash of blue rushing past her. She spun around to follow it, slipping on the leaves and grasping at tree trunks to steady herself.

"Wait!" she said, for she could see it racing ahead of her. She thought she could hear its breathing, and she could see that it truly was glowing like a light. If only it slowed down she would be able to get a better look at the sort of animal it was.

Something pulled her back, and with a wince she realized that her sleeve had caught on a branch and ripped halfway off its seam. Mrs. Mannerd would be furious; she made that slicker herself when the old one finally wore beyond all use. It was the only new article of clothing any of the children had been given this year.

Perhaps she could repair it before the morning and not be caught, Marybeth thought. Water seeping in through the tear, she ran on, her lungs burning in her chest. Lightning made the woods bright as day for an instant.

"Wait!" Too late, she felt the ground disappear from under her feet and realized that she had run into the river. The lantern flew from her hand, the candle extinguished the moment before she hit the water.

The darkness was so absolute, so silent, that at first Marybeth thought she was dead. It was the ache in her lungs that assured her she was still living, and she thrashed blindly for the surface, but there was no telling the surface from the depths in all that black.

And then she saw the blue light, and forgot her own hunger for air. She forgot to panic. Forgot that death was a possibility at all.

The light circled around her, long and soft like a tail. Its face came close to hers. It had a pointed snout like the foxes that ran through the woods, but its eyes were big and white, as though they were completely blank. Only when she stared harder did Marybeth see that there were faint silver pupils. The blue creature was studying her; was it trying to help?

She felt her eyes closing, her body floating off somewhere. Out of the river, away from the trees and the little red house, into a sky without stars in it.

Something hit her chest, hard. Warmth surged through her blood and, with it, the strength and the mind to kick herself up to the surface.

She broke through the water with a gasp.

The blue creature was gone.

CHAPTER
3

Lionel descended the stairs for breakfast ten minutes late, with his sandy brown hair not brushed and his shirt missing, as usual. The consequence was that he would miss out on a fresh bowl of oatmeal and toast, which he hardly minded. He would crawl about under the table looking for crusts the older ones dropped so Mrs. Mannerd would think them eaten. Sometimes there was still jam on them.

This morning, though, Mrs. Mannerd stood at the head of the table, wringing her apron and frowning.

"Tell the truth," she said, and Lionel could hear the worry in her voice. She didn't sound angry, which made the worry even louder. "Did you and Marybeth sneak out to play one of your games last night?"

Only then did Lionel realize that Marybeth's seat at the table was empty. Her bowl had been scraped clean, her toast snatched away by the older ones.

Lionel was not one to answer Mrs. Mannerd's questions, and he especially hated talking in the morning, when his voice cracked and his head was still filled with sleep. But he could feel Marybeth's absence. He could sense that she had left some trail that led out of this house and then disappeared.

"No," he said. His cracked voice sounded like it belonged to a little boy, and he hated how human it was.

Mrs. Mannerd knelt down before him. She took his hands—something she had never done. Lionel felt cornered, and he resisted the instinct to growl. "I need to know the truth," she said. Her eyes were small and startled. She was not an old woman anymore, but a bird that had lost one of her young and needed to find it before the weasel ate it for lunch.

Her grip on Lionel's hands tightened. His breathing became shallow; his pupils dilated; he could hear the older ones scraping the porridge from their bowls, the sounds they made becoming louder and closer, their chatter reduced to the grunting of pigs at a trough.

He saw that Marybeth's yellow slicker was missing from its hook.

"Please," Mrs. Mannerd said. Her entire face became the face of a bird.

Lionel ripped his hands from her grasp and ran for the door.

"Lionel!" Mrs. Mannerd cried. "For heaven's sake, this is important! I need you to be a rational child for once."

He was already out the door by then. Barefoot, he ran down the path that led into the woods. Marybeth had gone this way hours earlier. He followed the imprint of her boots.

The autumn air was cold and sharp against his bare skin. He paid the cold no mind, though, and imagined that he had grown a thick layer of fur like the coyotes that lived here even when there was snow.

He found a mark in the mud where Marybeth's heel had skidded. A flash of yellow caught his eye—thread from her slicker caught on a branch and fluttering.

Lionel willed his ear canals to expand so that he could listen for her. If she was hurt, she would be calling for help, and he would find her. He had to.

There was no sound. Lionel crawled on all fours, his ear close to the ground, listening.

The smell of rust caused his nostrils to flare. There in a bed of wet leaves, at the river's edge, was the lantern from the hall closet. Panicked, Lionel scrambled toward the water and looked inside. The water was so clear that he could see all the way down to the pebbles and roots at the bottom.

Marybeth's trail had come to a stop.

"Lionel!" He became aware that Mrs. Mannerd had been calling after him the whole time. Her voice was a screech. As she approached he heard the flutter of her bird wings.

But when she finally caught up to him, panting, he looked up and saw that she was human. "For heaven's sake," she wheezed, "I can't have you out here catching your death and—"

She saw the lantern resting on the ground beside where Lionel was crouched. Splatters of fresh wax were on its glass door. She looked at the river. "Oh," she breathed. "Lionel, come away from there. Get back inside the house."

He shook his head. This was the spot where Marybeth disappeared, and he could not leave until he knew what had happened to her. He was the only one who ever heard her gentle voice over all the commotion in the red house. He had found her in the summer when one of the older ones locked her in the closet, because he was the only one listening. He had smelled the salt of her tears even from several rooms away. If he left now, she would just disappear. No one would find her.

"Come on, Lionel."

His fingers and toes bore into the mud like claws.

Mrs. Mannerd grabbed the lantern with one hand and Lionel's wrist with the other. He screamed. She pulled him away from the river, and his frenzied kicks disturbed Marybeth's trail. The path she had taken last night was covered over with wet leaves. Gone. She was just gone.

The police came. Lionel was huddled in Marybeth's bed, his face pressed to the window, watching them. They ran through the trees with their bloodhounds on leashes.

Lionel's breath fogged the glass. He was trapped in a terrarium. This window was painted shut. Mrs. Mannerd had barricaded the door with a chair and told him to stay put. She couldn't have another child running off into the great unknown.

Downstairs, the older ones were chattering as they cleaned the house, stepping on every creaky floorboard and slamming the cabinet doors as they put away the dishes. Sunday was chore day, and Lionel could smell the soapy mop water. Whatever had happened the night before, all traces of it were gone from the house now.

He didn't think that something had come into the house to take Marybeth away. He would have known. He knew everything that came into the house. He knew where the mice nested in the walls because he could hear them skittering. But he wouldn't tell Mrs. Mannerd about them because she would try to kill them.

Before the police came and Mrs. Mannerd barricaded him in this room (it was the only one with a window that didn't open), he had crawled through the house, sniffing the floorboards and looking for bits of fur or strange footprints. But he was now very sure that she had left the house on her own, and that no one had been with her.

In the distance, he saw the bloodhounds investigating the water's edge. The bloodhounds were as perplexed as Lionel. They paced the river and pawed at the dirt.

When the police returned to the house, Lionel climbed from the bed and pressed his ear to the vent in the floor. He heard Mrs. Mannerd saying, "Not like her, not at all."

"These types of children run away sometimes, ma'am. They always turn up." The policeman's voice was like a growling dog. Lionel could imagine his yellowed teeth, could smell his hot breath.

"I know my children," Mrs. Mannerd said, still squawking like a frightened bird. "Marybeth wouldn't run away. Not her."

"Does she have any family? Any relations she may have been in contact with?"

"The girl lost her mother when she was born, and her

father died of tuberculosis in a sanatorium four—n-no—
five, it was five years ago now. She's been with us since
then."

It was the first time Lionel had ever heard Marybeth's
story. She had arrived at the little red house one soft,
snowy afternoon without explanation, as if she had fallen
from the sky.

More muffled words were spoken downstairs, and then
the police had gone.

Mrs. Mannerd came upstairs with a bowl of potato
stew and a slice of bread, which she set on the floor before
Lionel. She sat on the floor across from him, groaning as
she eased herself onto the boards.

Lionel hugged his knees and watched her. She still
looked worried, which perplexed him. Since Mr. Mannerd's passing, Mrs. Mannerd spent a great deal of time
griping about all the mouths she was left to feed alone, all
the footprints she had to wipe, the banging on the bathroom door when the bathwater had been running for too
long. Lionel did not expect that she would care especially
that one of her charges was missing.

"Listen to me," she said. "I didn't want to lock you in
this room, but I can't have you out there looking for her.
The police will look for her instead. You understand that,
don't you? If there's something dangerous out there, I
want you in here so you don't get hurt."

"The animals won't hurt me," Lionel said. They never had. He had even begun to earn the trust of the coyotes. They didn't come out for him yet, but he could feel them watching him when he crept out on the nights he was able to steal some meat from the refrigerator.

"I'm not talking about the animals," Mrs. Mannerd said, and her eyes turned watery and she clasped her hand over her mouth, as if she could stuff the words back onto her tongue and swallow them down.

But it was too late for that. Lionel already understood. He could make the chickens lay eggs and he could reason with the most stubborn of foxes. But he had learned years ago that humans were more dangerous than the things that stalked about in the wilderness.

CHAPTER 4

The sun had begun to set when the policeman knocked on the door. Mrs. Mannerd was scolding the older ones about their squabbling as she made her way to the door. When she opened it, the smell of baked beans and boiled potatoes wafted out into the chilly air.

Marybeth stood at the policeman's side, lilting sleepily and wearing a wool blanket over her slicker. Her hair was tangled and full of bits of leaves.

Mrs. Mannerd let out a cry.

"A woman up the road found her sleeping in their barn this afternoon. Would have returned her sooner, but she wouldn't tell us where she lived."

"Marybeth!" Mrs. Mannerd said, and knelt before her. "Why on earth not?"

"I couldn't remember," Marybeth said.

"Come in, come in, before you freeze. I can't thank you enough, Officer, really."

Mrs. Mannerd and the policeman were still talking when Marybeth kicked out of her boots and moved into the house. She walked as though she were floating, past the kitchen where the older ones were playing cards and betting their chores, up the stairs to where Lionel had been watching her from between the rungs of the bannister.

His face was splashed with freckles that came from his countless hours spent in the sun, his eyes wide and dark. As she climbed the steps, he crawled out of the shadows and sat on the landing to greet her.

He was waiting for an explanation, Marybeth supposed. But all she said was, "You ought to be wearing a shirt. It's cold." She knelt beside him and wrapped the wool blanket around his shoulders. The gesture was so very like her, and so familiar, that Lionel felt an aching in his chest. This was still Marybeth, but something had changed. Something she wasn't telling him.

He didn't know how to ask her what was different. He had never had to ask her anything. Marybeth was uncomplicated on the surface. Predictable. But Lionel knew when anything was amiss, and he had always known how to fix it.

When she was sad, he could bring her to the river and lure the fish to the surface to dance for them. When she was angry, he raced her, until they had run so far from the little red house and were so out of breath that they collapsed into the grass and laughed.

But for once, he didn't know where she had been, or what had changed, or how to fix it.

As she moved to stand, he said, "Wait."

She stayed in place, and he leaned forward, squinting at her gnarled brown hair and then at her face. "Where are your spectacles?"

She blinked. "Aren't I wearing them?"

Lionel shook his head.

Marybeth brought her hands to her temples. "Oh. I suppose I don't need them anymore." She stood, and as she walked toward her room, she did not look back to see his perplexed eyes blinking after her. She did not see that he was gnawing on his lip.

Marybeth did not come downstairs for supper. Still wearing her yellow slicker, she climbed up to her bunk and slept until Mrs. Mannerd opened the door and filled the dark room with light from the hallway. She was carrying a tray of stew and bread, which she set on the desk the children used for their schoolwork.

"Are you asleep? Didn't you get enough sleep in the barn?" She was being facetious, of course.

Marybeth raised her head sleepily from the pillow. She was finding it difficult to keep her eyes open.

Mrs. Mannerd didn't see Lionel lurking behind her and peering at Marybeth from behind her faded gingham dress. Marybeth saw him, but only for a moment before Mrs. Mannerd came in and closed the door behind her.

"Come down now and eat something," Mrs. Mannerd said, and it occurred to Marybeth that she was hungry. She felt as though she hadn't eaten in years.

She sat at the desk and began spooning the stew into her mouth greedily, as Mrs. Mannerd plucked the leaves from her hair.

"Are you ready to talk about what happened?" Mrs. Mannerd said.

"'What happened'?" Marybeth asked.

"What happened that led to you falling asleep in a barn. Was one of the children mean to you again?"

Marybeth continued eating her stew, giving no care to stop the splatters from getting on her sleeves. She shrugged. It was most unlike her, and Mrs. Mannerd wrung her hands and fretted. She noticed the torn sleeve but didn't remark on it. She would mend it later.

"Marybeth, has someone hurt you?"

"No."

"You're certain?"

Marybeth didn't answer. She was too busy eating the stew, pausing only to take bites from the bread.

Most unlike her, Mrs. Mannerd thought.

When Mrs. Mannerd left the room, she saw Lionel crouched by the door. She thought that he might do something wild, but he didn't. He looked up at her, and in his wide eyes Mrs. Mannerd saw only sorrow.

"There now, it's all right," she told him. "Have you eaten? There's some extra bread and butter in the kitchen."

She held out her hand, and for once he took it. It was rare that he let her stand this close, much less reached out to touch her. In her pity, and in his fear, for once they had some common ground.

Marybeth had always been a child who blended into the wallpaper and the wood grain, but without her red spectacles, she became even more invisible. The older ones shoved past her on their way downstairs to the breakfast table, jostling her about. Marybeth didn't seem to mind this either. She walked with an eerie poise, as though she were carrying something breakable on her head.

Lionel was at the table early for once. He hadn't overslept; he had been awake all night. He rarely worried, but when he did, it made him nocturnal like the coyotes and spiders.

He sat at a chair so that he could keep an eye on Mary-beth, and he didn't acknowledge Mrs. Mannerd's words of encouragement and praise as she spooned oatmeal into his bowl.

Marybeth had not bothered with her braids this morning, and Lionel could see how long her hair truly was. It disappeared under the table, straight and smooth like the ribbons that hung on spools in the tailor shop window.

She stared down at her bowl and drew patterns in the oatmeal, her mouth pensively puckered off to one side.

"Too slow!" one of the older ones, a boy, shouted as he reached across the table for her toast and jam.

He was a boy that Lionel had long ago decided was a hyena, and when he had told Marybeth she had agreed. He had large ears, small eyes, and hunched shoulders.

As the hyena boy bit into the toast and let out a taunt-ing "Mmmmm," he did not see the sudden, vicious glare in Marybeth's eyes. He did not hear her low growl.

In an instant, Marybeth had scrambled over the table, knocking over glasses of milk and scattering the bowls, and she bit the hyena boy in the neck.

He let out a cry, but Marybeth had latched onto him. She kept her teeth in his skin even as he pulled at her hair and fell backward onto the floor with a crash. By the time Mrs. Mannerd grabbed the collar of Marybeth's dress

and pulled her away, the hyena boy was in tears. Blood was trailing from his neck. "She bit me! The little brat bit me!"

Startled, Marybeth looked around the dining room. All the children were staring at her now. The hyena boy's blood stained her lips, and she was breathing hard.

"Marybeth," Mrs. Mannerd gasped, but before she could get a good look at Marybeth, she was gone. She ran from the dining room, through the kitchen, and outside, forgetting her shoes and coat; the storm door slammed shut behind her.

Lionel had been the only one looking at her the moment before she lunged, and he was the only one who saw the flash of blue in her irises.

He ran after her. Mrs. Mannerd threw her hands up in exasperation, muttering that those two would be the death of her one of these days.

Lionel was not going to let Marybeth disappear this time. He kept his sight on her maroon dress and its white sailor collar that fluttered behind her. He caught up to her when she at last stopped at the river's edge.

She sat on the big rock, hugged her knees to her chest, and buried her face in them.

Lionel approached cautiously. He crawled with his belly low to the rock, and then he sat across from her. He didn't speak, only watched her with his head canted.

"I didn't mean it," she finally said, her voice muffled. "I didn't want to bite him."

"It's okay that you did," Lionel said. He could hear the distress in her voice, and it caused him a great deal of pain. "He took your toast. Eagles will fight to the death over something like that."

"I'm not an eagle, Lionel. I'm a girl." She looked at him. Her eyes were their usual brown again. There was still blood in the corner of her mouth. "I'm a girl."

Lionel had never seen her this way before. Whenever the humans in the house were upset, he made a habit of avoiding them. One of the things he liked about Mary-beth was that she was never upset. They both had an animalistic approach to things, he thought. They survived and didn't bother with the emotional nonsense.

But now that she was upset, he could not avoid her the way he avoided the others.

Slowly, he crawled beside her and patted her shoulder. "I don't think you bit him very hard," he said.

"There's something wrong with me." She looked at him. "The night before last, I saw the blue animal from my bedroom window. I tried to wake you, but I couldn't. So I went out alone. I chased it all the way to the river."

Lionel thought back to the trail he had followed when he searched for her, and now he understood. The yellow

threads, the dropped lantern. That's what she had been doing out there.

"I fell into the river, and I couldn't find my way out," she went on. "It came in after me. I think—I think it jumped inside my skin."

Lionel looked at her bare arms, welled with gooseflesh from the cold. "I don't see it."

She shook her head. "It can't be seen. But it's still there. I feel it. I think—I think it wants to protect me. That's why it got so angry when one of the older ones took my food."

Lionel considered this. "There aren't many animals that burrow under the skin. Some insects, maybe. Did you get a good look at it?"

"Not very. It was underwater," Marybeth said. "It glowed."

"Could it have been the moonlight reflecting?" Lionel asked.

"It was cloudy. There was no moonlight. And, anyway, it couldn't have been something like that. It glowed like it was made of light itself." Without her spectacles, the fear in her eyes was that much more prominent. "Are there any animals that glow?"

"Jellyfish. But there aren't any in this river." Lionel shrugged. "Lightning bugs."

"It wasn't a jellyfish or lightning bugs," Marybeth said.

Lionel lay on his belly and dipped his head into the river. He saw nothing but minnows and roots and rocks. Water was dripping from his hair when he emerged. He hadn't found anything, but Marybeth already knew that he wouldn't.

"Don't worry." He looked just like a boy when he smiled at her. Marybeth was the only person in the world who ever got to see his human mannerisms. "Whatever it is, I've never met an animal I can't reach."

Marybeth wasn't consoled by this. She looked as though she might cry.

Lionel thought back to yesterday, that horrible moment when he saw the lantern by the river and thought she had fallen in. He thought he would look down and find her floating there with her lungs full of water, gone forever.

In that moment, he had known with certainty that if Marybeth had drowned, there would be nothing human left to him at all. He would have forgotten how to speak. He would not have been able to hear words—only angry growls coming out of human throats. Things like porridge and tables and houses would have been meaningless, and he would have disappeared into the darkest shadows of the trees.

But Marybeth was still alive, and so whatever happened next couldn't be too terrible to fix.

He ambled back up to her side. "I'll help you," he said.

Some of the tension eased from her frame, and she rested her head against his shoulder.

"Oh, Lionel," she said, very softly. "How?"

CHAPTER
5

The older ones attended school in town, and they had left the house by the time Lionel and Marybeth returned.

Mrs. Mannerd was scrubbing dishes at the kitchen sink, and when she saw the pair of them shuffle through the door, she sighed. "The tutor will be here in an hour. Just this once, do you think the two of you can get through your lessons without howling at the moon or biting anyone?"

"It's morning," Lionel said. "There is no moon."

"Heaven knows that hasn't stopped you before. Brush your hair, both of you. You look a mess."

For Marybeth's sake, Lionel behaved during their lessons. He drank the glass of orange juice Mrs. Mannerd brought him, and he didn't purr or twitch his nose even once when the tutor complimented his poise.

But just because he didn't behave like an animal did not mean he didn't listen like one. As he and Marybeth sat across from each other at the dining room table working on their fractions, he listened to Mrs. Mannerd and the tutor whispering in the kitchen.

He put his hand over Marybeth's pencil to still it.

She raised her head.

"Shh," he said. The pencil's scratching against the page was making it harder to hear.

Marybeth only heard murmuring, while Lionel heard the words being spoken.

"Something awful happened to that little girl out there," Mrs. Mannerd said. "You should have seen the way she lunged at Marcus during breakfast."

"Do you suppose someone took her?" the tutor asked.

"I can't get her to say two words about it. But she's different. I can see it on her face. She's lost her spectacles, and now suddenly she swears she doesn't need them."

"Whatever did happen, you must handle it delicately," the tutor said.

Lionel looked at Marybeth, who was twirling her pencil between her fingers, waiting to get back to her homework. "What is it?" she whispered.

"You have to act normal," Lionel whispered back.

For the rest of the morning, Marybeth did just that. She spoke softly, and after her lessons she sat outside, her face half-covered by her scarf as she read through a stack of encyclopedias, looking up as many animals as she could think of. She studied the details of the sketches and looked for something that resembled what she'd seen in the river, but there was nothing.

When she began to grow frustrated and scared, she felt the blue creature's heart beating in her chest right beside her own, and felt oddly soothed by it.

She came inside only when she was called to supper. Lionel was not permitted to read the encyclopedias for another week, but he was allowed to help Marybeth carry them inside and arrange them on the shelf that was built into the staircase.

During supper, Mrs. Mannerd saw the tension between Marybeth and Lionel versus the older ones and she declared that nobody was allowed to speak, and any child to utter so much as a burp would be sent to bed with an empty stomach.

The hyena boy glared at Marybeth, but she paid him no mind. She had been feeling hungrier than usual all evening, and now that she had food, she was ravenous.

Lionel, who had brought his plate under the table, handed Marybeth his buttered bread. He would have

given her his slice of meatloaf, which he was never going to eat despite Mrs. Mannerd's best efforts, but one of the older ones had stepped on it.

After dinner, Mrs. Mannerd lit a fire and sat in her wingchair to knit scarves with the yarn she'd found at the consignment shop.

The older ones were upstairs, fighting about who got to use the bathroom and who had been standing in front of the mirror for too long.

Usually, Lionel would be hiding somewhere. It made him very nervous to be in the house when it was filled with children, and he had a way of blending into the wallpaper.

But since Marybeth's return, he had become like her shadow, Mrs. Mannerd noticed. He followed Marybeth as she made her way to the fireplace and sat on the floor with some scrap paper and a pencil.

Marybeth lay on her stomach and began to sketch. Lionel curled up beside her like a cat, his eyes following the movement of her hand as it went.

Mrs. Mannerd looked up from her yarn. "What are you drawing?"

"A kite," Marybeth said.

It was a sensible drawing for a sensible girl, Mrs. Mannerd thought. At last things were returning to normal.

There was a loud crash upstairs, and Mrs. Mannerd grumbled. Before she could take so much as a breath to ask what happened, she heard the children arguing over whose fault it was.

With a sigh, she set down her knitting and made her way up the creaky stairs.

Lionel was still watching Marybeth. Her fingers tightened around the pencil, and her arm trembled, as though she was fighting to keep control over it.

"Marybeth?" he whispered.

When he looked at her eyes, they were blue.

He sat up slowly. "Marybeth." At once his tone was a coo, the way he talked to the fat mother rabbit.

Her head twitched in his direction. She was in there, fighting for control.

"It's all right," Lionel said. "Listen to my voice. Come back to me." He didn't dare allow himself to sound frightened.

Marybeth drew a shaky breath. She tilted her head down low, so that her hair covered her face. The pencil in her hand began to move.

Lionel kept a wary distance, and he watched as Marybeth's practiced drawing of a kite transformed into something that resembled a face, with dark eyes staring through a murky haze.

Then, the pencil dropped. It rolled across the floor and gently hit the brick fireplace.

Marybeth's face was still hidden. Lionel inched toward her—slowly, slowly—and reached for the paper.

But the blue creature was faster. It snatched the paper from the floor and threw it into the fire. Its edges curled up immediately. The face was still staring out as it burned.

Marybeth was close, too close, to the flame. Still with that eerie blue gleam in her eye, she held her hand out to the fire.

Lionel grabbed her hand. The blue creature snarled and hissed and tried to bite him, but just this once he was faster. He wrapped his arms around Marybeth's elbows and pinned her back against his chest.

The blue creature within her howled like a wolf caught in a snare.

"Marybeth!" he said. "Come back."

He knew that she had heard him when the tension left her body. She awoke, breathing hard. "Lionel?" It was Marybeth's voice. No blue fox or other creature could ever duplicate that.

She began to tremble, and he didn't let go of her. "It's all right," he said. He didn't know if that was true, but the words didn't matter. It was all in the tone. None of the wild creatures spoke a word of English, and yet he communicated to them in much the same way.

"It's trying to tell me something." Marybeth was trying not to cry. "It wants me to know something."

"Know what?"

"I'm not sure," she said. "Something terrible. Maybe it's a trick. Maybe it's trying to kill me."

"I won't let it," Lionel said. "I'll always help you find your way back."

They watched the paper burn to nothing, and he didn't tell her that he was starting to truly feel afraid.

Mrs. Mannerd returned to her knitting, muttering something about the children always breaking the few valuables she owned.

Marybeth sat huddled by the fire, with her eyes fixed on the flame.

"What happened to your pretty drawing, Marybeth?" Mrs. Mannerd asked.

Marybeth winced, as though the question had awoken her from a dream.

"I ate it," Lionel said. He was sitting beside her. "It wasn't a pretty drawing. It was bark, and I needed it to survive the winter."

Mrs. Mannerd was looking at him closely. This did not seem like one of his typical games. Rather than the usual mischief she normally saw in his eyes, there was

ferocity. And she almost could believe that he was a wild
thing, protecting its family against the cruel darkness of
night.

At bedtime, Lionel grabbed his blanket and slept huddled by Marybeth's bedroom door. If he had gone with
Marybeth the night of the storm, none of this would
have ever happened, and he would not let her down
again.

Hours passed, and late into the night, the clatter of
Mrs. Mannerd's sewing machine came to a stop.

When at last everyone in the house was asleep, Lionel
was awoken by the creak of a floorboard and he opened
his eyes.

Marybeth was halfway down the stairs, and from the
moonlight in the window he could just see the outline
of her white nightgown. He followed after her on all
fours—he could be much quieter that way—and watched
as she moved for the front door.

"Wait," he whispered.

Marybeth spun around. For a second her eyes glowed
blue. She hissed, startled.

Lionel knew better than to approach all at once. He
knew that the blue creature did not yet trust him as well
as Marybeth did.

"I was only going to say that you'll need your coat." He rose to his feet and edged along with his back pressed against the wall, as far away from her as he could be. When he reached the tattered wool coat that hung by the door with all the other coats, he removed it and held it with his arm extended.

The blue creature eyed it warily. Lionel tossed it onto the floor at Marybeth's feet and hoped that the creature could be reasoned with.

He did not like to see those blue eyes on Marybeth's face. He did not like the unknowing stare they gave.

Eventually, it took the coat. It had no trouble putting it on and buttoning it, which Lionel found peculiar. What sort of animal was this blue creature that it knew how to dress itself? Several years ago, there was a feral cat that birthed a litter of kittens behind the shed where Mr. Mannerd used to make furniture. One of the older ones had knit a sweater for one of the more docile kittens, and when she had tried to put the sweater on the kitten, it nearly tore the nose from her face.

The creature turned the doorknob.

"You'll need shoes," Lionel said. He was thinking of the gooseflesh on Marybeth's skin that afternoon; she could not tolerate the cold weather as well as he could.

The blue creature wriggled Marybeth's feet into her

boots and stepped out into the windy autumn air. Lionel followed several feet behind.

He followed the blue creature across the front lawn, down the long dirt driveway that led to the road, and then down the road itself. For as long as he could remember, Marybeth had been the one who followed him at a distance, never wanting to disturb the animals he sought as company. He wondered how she could stand it. It was horribly lonely watching her from afar; the creature didn't look over her shoulder at him.

He wondered if Marybeth had any say in where they were going.

After what Lionel guessed had been a mile, the creature in Marybeth's skin turned off the road and down a grassy hill. Lionel followed.

There was an old farmhouse in the distance. All its windows were dark. Marybeth would never trespass, and so it was strange to watch her stride so confidently past the house, through the yard, to the barn that didn't sound as though it contained any animals.

Lionel followed the blue creature into the barn, to where the moonlight no longer reached them. There were mice skittering behind the hay bales. Marybeth was a coward around mice and would have backed away, but the blue creature was undeterred. It made a bed for itself in the dirt and curled up there.

Lionel would have thought the blue creature had gone to sleep, but he could still see that foreign blue glow in Marybeth's opened eyes. The blue creature was watching him. Lionel crouched to the ground and held out his hand. Marybeth's nostrils flared as the blue creature sniffed him.

"What are you?" Lionel asked, more to himself than to the creature. The creature was not violent, but he didn't like that it had hidden Marybeth away somewhere. Her body was right in front of him, but she was as gone as she had been the other day when he found the lantern by the river.

"Will you come out?" he said. "Your coat was so lovely and blue. I'd like to see it again."

The creature closed its eyes and slept.

Once Lionel was sure that the blue creature would not awaken, he took Marybeth's wrist and held his fingers to her pulse point. He felt Marybeth's heart throbbing gently, as the hearts of humans did. But beside that heartbeat he felt another that galloped like hooves against the hard ground.

All night Lionel sat beside Marybeth and the blue creature and kept watch. He was still awake when the rooster crowed and the morning light began to fill the cracks in the barn walls. He had been watching Marybeth's sleeping face, trying to determine which one of

them was in control. Sometimes her lip would pull back in a snarl, and always the eyebrows were drawn together. Even in sleep her face was troubled.

He shook Marybeth's shoulder. He knew that the blue creature was still wary of him and he didn't want to anger it, but Mrs. Mannerd would be awake soon and wondering where they'd gone.

Marybeth's body stirred. She cringed when the smell of the barn reached her. It was like mold and old manure. She pushed herself upright, blinking, and Lionel could see that she was Marybeth again. The cold hit her all at once, and her lip shook as she shivered. "Am I dreaming?"

"No," Lionel said. "I followed you here. We have to go back now." It was strange even to him that he should be the voice of reason, but Marybeth wasn't entirely herself these days and he didn't want Mrs. Mannerd locking her in the house.

Marybeth staggered to her feet and grasped a hay bale for support. She started walking for the door.

Lionel followed her.

"I remember this," she said. "I thought I was dreaming."

Her eyes were no longer blue. They were familiar, but still Lionel sensed there was something that wasn't right about the way she stared ahead.

She walked out into the chilly morning air. She stopped to look at the farmhouse. It was small and colonial, with a tattered wooden fence whose paint was stripped down to mossy wood.

Lionel stared at it, too. But he did not understand what about it had captured Marybeth's attention. It was not very different from the red house where they lived, or any of the other houses they'd passed on their way here.

Marybeth didn't walk toward the house, though. Instead, she walked even farther from the main road, until she had led them to a river overrun with weeds.

"This is the river that runs all the way to our house," she said. "I've seen it when Mrs. Mannerd takes us into town. I asked her once, and she said it ran clean through the entire state." Her breath came out in little clouds. "The water must be freezing cold, but when I fell in, I didn't feel cold at all."

"What did you feel?" Lionel asked.

"Frightened, at first," Marybeth said. "It was strange. All in one second I thought, 'I'm never going to be old like Mrs. Mannerd. The veins in my hands will never look like maps.'"

Lionel looked at Marybeth's hands. They were starting to turn blue from the cold. She knelt at the water's edge and looked inside. "I never thought about how dangerous water was before. It seems so pretty and harmless. How many other pretty things are dangerous, do you suppose?"

"Anything can be dangerous," Lionel said. He turned his head at the sound of a door squeaking. Someone was coming out of the farmhouse. He grabbed Marybeth's arm and tried to pull her toward the trees so that they could hide.

She resisted. There was a flash of blue in her eyes, and when she hissed, it was so fierce that Lionel let go. He backed two steps away. If the creature was in charge, he didn't want it to run away in fear, nor did he want it to attack him.

But Marybeth came back immediately this time, and her face went pale. "Lionel? I—" She sobbed.

"Oh, no no no, don't cry," Lionel said eagerly. "It's all right. I shouldn't have gotten so close. I won't do it again." He was finding it difficult to do all this talking. He spoke to Marybeth more than he spoke to anyone, but even with her he didn't have to do it often. But now, with this untrusting creature under her skin, he would have to learn to use his words before he acted. "Someone is coming. We can hide in those trees."

It was too late, though. A voice called from the top of the embankment, "What are you children doing by that river? Don't you know you could drown?"

CHAPTER
6

At the kitchen table in the farmhouse, Marybeth ate the scrambled eggs like she'd never seen food before. She even drank Lionel's milk, not that he minded. He was too busy trying to act human to be bothered with breakfast. He sat at the table and tried to find a place to rest his hands.

The old woman chuckled at this. "If you're going to keep coming back here, I'll have to get another cow for milk."

This was the second time Marybeth had spent the night in that barn, and the second time the old woman made her breakfast. The old woman didn't seem to mind. Unlike Mrs. Mannerd, she did not have a house filled with children asking for things, and she had a great many things to give. Her pantry was full, and it was a big house.

"Don't you want your eggs?" the old woman asked Lionel.

He shook his head.

"What's the matter, cat got your tongue?"

"No, thank you," he said. The words stuck in his throat.

"He likes to eat things he finds outside," Marybeth said. "There are berry bushes by our house."

"You have to be careful with those," the old woman said. "Lots of berries are poison."

"Lionel always knows the difference." She smiled across the table at him, and Lionel wished that the creature, whatever it was, would leave her. She was acting like herself this morning, but last night the animal had once again given Lionel cause to be afraid. He wasn't afraid that the animal would harm him, but rather that it would take over completely, and Marybeth would be gone.

"Eat up," the old woman said. "I'll take you home. Your mother must be worried sick."

"Yes, thank you," Marybeth said. She didn't correct the old woman and say that Mrs. Mannerd wasn't her mother.

Marybeth did her best to look the part of a normal girl. She brushed her teeth and kept them pearly white, and she braided her hair, and she said "please" and "thank you." But normal girls had mothers, and there was nothing she could do to make up for that. All she could do was play along when people assumed that she had one.

The sound of footsteps caused Lionel to tense. His nostrils flared, and all at once he smelled something similar to the air inside the barn.

Across the table, Marybeth raised her head. Her pupils dilated, like an animal that had just been startled. Lionel watched her. Even when the creature wasn't in charge, she was becoming less like a girl and more like a wild thing herself.

The footsteps came down the stairs, which groaned and creaked as though someone were trying to pry off their boards. Marybeth shrank in her chair. She set down her fork and hid her hands under the table.

When the man entered the kitchen, Marybeth's tension didn't ease up, even though the man looked perfectly ordinary. He wore pinstriped pajamas and had messy hair. He saw Lionel and Marybeth at the table, and he said, "What's this?"

"I've found children in the barn again," the old woman said. "Two of them this time."

"Well, you can't keep them," the man said. "Take them back."

"I know that," the old woman said. She looked at Lionel and Marybeth and said, "This is my son, Reginald. He forgets his manners in the mornings."

Marybeth stared at her plate. Her appetite was gone.

"Are you all done?" the old woman said. "Come on, then, I'll give you a lift back home. That is, if you remember where it is this time."

There was a low growl in Marybeth's throat, like the one she'd given before she lunged on the hyena boy, but only Lionel heard it.

"I remember where we live," he said.

Marybeth stood, and Lionel followed her at a close distance. Something was troubling her and he would have liked to hold her hand, but he was afraid of summoning the blue creature again. And he couldn't ask her what was the matter, not with the old woman around.

The old woman led them to a green pickup truck that was parked on the grass. "Didn't learn to use this contraption until my Abner died, God rest his soul," the old woman said.

Mrs. Mannerd was running out of the little red house even before the truck had made it down the driveway. Lionel did his best to make himself into an opossum; he did not care to do any more speaking.

"Oh, Marybeth, not again," Mrs. Mannerd said, when Marybeth and Lionel climbed out of the car.

The old woman stepped out of the car. She had a very kind face, and it seemed to put Mrs. Mannerd at ease. The old woman was not the sort of dangerous person Mrs. Mannerd had warned Lionel about. "I do apologize," Mrs. Mannerd said. "I don't know what has gotten into these two. They've never wandered off like this before."

"It was no trouble," the old woman said, and despite her smile Lionel could sense that she was sad. "It's nice having children on the farm again, even if only for a quick breakfast."

"That's very generous, but they won't be troubling you again. Lionel, Marybeth, in the house."

Marybeth hesitated. There was something about the old woman that she liked. She was staring at her face and trying to think of what it was.

"Come on," Lionel said.

He began walking toward the house, and Marybeth followed him just as she always did.

CHAPTER
7

As she moved about the kitchen preparing for breakfast, Mrs. Mannerd told Mr. Porter that she was coming to her wit's end. "That Lionel is one thing," she said. "He's never been quite right, but even he never ran away before all of this. And now Marybeth! My only bit of sanity among the lot of these children has lost her marbles."

Lionel and Marybeth were huddled together with their ears pressed to the floor vent in the girls' bedroom, listening.

Marybeth sat up and leaned against the wall. "It's true," she said. "I am losing my marbles. I walked that whole way to the farm, and I thought I was dreaming it." She looked at Lionel. "What if I wander somewhere more dangerous next?"

"It always seems to be that barn," Lionel said. "Maybe the blue creature likes hay."

"We have our own barn here," Marybeth said.

"Ours has animals in it," Lionel said. "Maybe the blue creature likes to be alone."

Marybeth shook her head. "There's something about that barn. And that old woman." Her breaths came quicker. The difference was slight, but Lionel noticed. "And that man."

Marybeth hadn't braided her hair for days now, and she began to tug at a piece of it. She was thinking of the man—the old woman's son—but she didn't have the words to describe what the thought of him did to her nerves. She felt a heart begin to pound in her chest, and she knew that the heart was not her own.

It was Tuesday. Errand day. It was the one day of the week that Mrs. Mannerd was allowed any reprieve from the children, or so she liked to say.

But that morning, once the older ones had gone off to school, she told Lionel and Marybeth, "Get your coats. You're coming into town with me."

"What about our lessons?" Marybeth asked.

"They'll resume tomorrow." Mrs. Mannerd did not like to interfere with the children's education; with no parents and no inheritance to help them get by, they would need their brains. But she worried at the thought of leaving that poor tutor alone with Marybeth in her current state, wandering off as she had begun to. Lionel was no help. He would only follow her, if he weren't too busy gnawing on the table legs like a beaver.

Lionel and Marybeth followed Mrs. Mannerd out to the car. It was a Cadillac that used to be the color of a manzanilla olive but now resembled a rust-spotted Dalmatian, and it was old and took several turns in the ignition before it sparked to life.

"Marybeth," Mrs. Mannerd said as she backed the car down the long dirt driveway. "Why don't you put those pretty braids in your hair anymore?"

"I forgot," Marybeth said.

Mrs. Mannerd caught Marybeth's eyes in the mirror. With her long hair fanning around her shoulders and without her spectacles, Marybeth looked like a different girl completely.

Mrs. Mannerd had found Marybeth's spectacles in the leaves near the river and was patiently waiting for Marybeth to admit she was nearsighted and ask to have them back. But if Marybeth was pretending to have perfect vision, she was doing a convincing job of it.

"If you children are on your best behavior with me today, I'll let you have a treat. How's that? I'll take you to the library and you can look at anything you'd like."

"Even the encyclopedias?" Lionel asked.

"I suppose it's been long enough," Mrs. Mannerd said. "As long as you promise not to pretend you're a lion and chase the children through the house again."

Lionel hadn't been pretending. On the afternoon that he had chosen to be a lion, he was merely trying to protect himself from the older ones when they had barricaded the door so he couldn't go outside to feed his wild rabbits. One small boy was no match for a herd of six monstrous baboons with fangs that extended to their chins when they laughed. Only a lion could best them.

But he knew that he could never make Mrs. Mannerd see reason, and so he said, "Yes, I promise."

"Well, all right then," Mrs. Mannerd said.

Marybeth nudged him. "Say thank you," she whispered.

Lionel made a sour face, and she nudged him again.

"Thank you, Mrs. Mannerd," he said. The words stuck to his tongue, and he fought the urge to hiss.

He saw the reflection of Mrs. Mannerd's raised eyebrows in the mirror. "You're most welcome, young man."

"I'm not a young man," Lionel said. "I'm going to grow up to be a leopard, or maybe a bear."

Mrs. Mannerd sighed.

Once they reached the center of town and stepped out of the car, Marybeth and Lionel truly did try their best to behave. Marybeth walked slowly and with poise; she didn't know what would cause the blue creature to awaken, and she didn't want to provoke it.

Lionel walked beside her, watching her with heightened senses, prepared to create a diversion if the blue creature did emerge.

"Come along," Mrs. Mannerd said. "Move your feet, pick it up. That's it."

In the tailor shop, there was a giant box of mismatched buttons. Lionel and Marybeth arranged them into patterns as Mrs. Mannerd ordered a bolt of fabric to repair the children's winter coats now that winter was coming.

Marybeth picked out all the blue buttons and the deep purples, and when Lionel noticed the concentration on her face, he stopped touching the buttons and he watched her. Her tongue peeked out from between her lips. Her eyes were big and dazed.

"Marybeth, what a lovely collage," Mrs. Mannerd said. Marybeth blinked, and then looked at her handiwork.

The buttons were arranged in the pattern of a blue painting whose shades and hues made up a face with blank spaces for eye sockets. Marybeth did not think it was lovely. She had no memory of making it whatsoever, and now that strange heart was beating in her chest again and she felt as though she might faint.

Lionel stared at the button face. Marybeth's pallor wasn't lost on him. He thought that the button face was as disturbing as any other portrait that lacked eyes, but beyond that it meant nothing to him. Whether the face was young or old, whether it belonged to a boy or to a girl, he couldn't say.

"Let's move along now," Mrs. Mannerd said. "We have other things to tend to." Marybeth was already at the door, eager to leave it behind.

As they walked from store to store, Lionel watched Marybeth. She had her head down and her arms crossed tight against her stomach. She looked frightened and horribly sad.

Lionel felt helpless. He couldn't talk about the blue creature or the button collage in front of Mrs. Mannerd. He would have liked to climb one of the trees along the sidewalk. He could dangle upside down by his knees and become a monkey. That would make her laugh for sure. But Mrs. Mannerd would not approve, and then she wouldn't take them to the library.

All he could do was whisper, "It'll be all right."

She turned her head sharply to him. Her eyes flashed blue for only a second, but even after they returned to their usual brown, the skepticism remained.

"Trust me," he said, to both Marybeth and the blue creature.

Marybeth looked at her boots. She nodded, just slightly.

Lionel wanted to be rid of this blue creature. He had never met an animal he didn't like, but he was growing to hate this one. Marybeth had always been soft spoken, but never subdued. He could see it in the way she walked. She was so worried about awakening the awful thing that she didn't even raise her eyes.

This blue creature was no different from the older ones who had locked her in the closet. But this time, he didn't know how to open the door and set her free.

By late morning, the car was filled with fabric and groceries, and there had been no outbursts or displays from either of the children. Lionel had done an impressive job behaving like a human, and Marybeth had not wandered off. So, as promised, Mrs. Mannerd took them to the library.

"We have an hour before it's time to go home for lunch," she said. "I'll be just over there." She pointed to a row of shelves near the door.

As Lionel and Marybeth climbed the spiral staircase that led to the library's top floor, Marybeth said, "There's no sense looking at the encyclopedias. We have them at home, and I've been through all of them. I must have looked up every animal that ever existed. Even the ones that have gone extinct."

"What next, then?" Lionel asked.

Marybeth peered over the railing at Mrs. Mannerd, who was browsing a traveler's atlas. "Come on." She led him past a row of empty tables and down a narrow aisle of books. "While I was researching, I found something that gave me an idea." She stopped walking, and Lionel looked up at the sign affixed above the bookshelf:

Supernatural Occurrences

He looked at Marybeth. "You think it's supernatural?"

"We've already ruled out everything else," she said. "There are animals that burrow and dig, but mostly in the ground. And there are parasites that can get under your skin, but they aren't as big as a fox, and they surely don't glow the way that this one did."

Lionel stared at the books, overwhelmed by all the dusty cloth spines and the possibilities they represented. He knew everything about animals and nothing about ghosts. "Where should we start?"

Marybeth shrugged. "Alphabetically, I suppose."

Lionel became an iguana and scaled the shelves so that he could reach the topmost books.

They sat on the floor, below a flickering bulb, and read passages aloud to each other as they researched. They read about photographers who took pictures of spirits, and spiritualists who could summon the dead and see the past.

"We don't have any money," Marybeth said. "Do you suppose they'd do it for free? If we explained?"

"No," Lionel said. "They'd want money. Especially if we explained."

Marybeth frowned at the page. "We could try to make money."

"I don't think it's a good idea," Lionel said. "I don't trust them, and, anyway, it looks fake to me. That ghost is wearing a trench coat. Why would a ghost wear a trench coat? Clothes are so itchy. If I were dead, I wouldn't wear anything."

Marybeth stared at the photo a long time, and then her eyes filled with tears.

"I'm sorry," Lionel said. He didn't want to make her cry. He wanted to yell at this blue creature to leave her alone. He had liked the old Marybeth, who was bright and inquisitive and never looked sad. He missed that Marybeth, and he wanted her back.

"It's not what you said," Marybeth sobbed. "It's not me. It's this." She grabbed his hand and brought it to her neck so that he could feel the pulse galloping beside her own. "It's telling me what to feel."

Lionel drew back. "What does it feel?"

Marybeth rubbed the tears from her eyes. "Home-sick. It's getting harder to tell what I'm feeling and what it's feeling, but I know this isn't me. I've never felt homesick."

"Does it want you to go back to the barn?"

"I don't know," she said. "I feel like I should growl at you, and climb that tree outside that window there and run off before Mrs. Mannerd catches me. But I know that I don't want to at the same time."

"Can you tell it to go away?" Lionel said.

"I've been trying. I don't think it wants to listen."

Mrs. Mannerd came up the steps, wheezing and muttering about her sore knees. "Children, it's time to get home and make lunch, and—my goodness, what are you doing in such a peculiar section?"

"We've read nearly everything else," Marybeth said politely. "Now we'd like to read about ghosts."

Mrs. Mannerd put her hands on her hips and looked at Lionel. "I suppose you're going to act like a ghost around the house now," she said.

"I'm not dead, so I can't be a ghost," Lionel said. He wouldn't know where to begin, and what would be the use? A ghost couldn't get the chickens to lay eggs or feed the coyotes.

On their way out, Marybeth and Lionel each borrowed a book from the Supernatural Occurrences section, and they were both very quiet on the drive home. Marybeth read, and Lionel petted the bolt of fabric like it was a lion cub. He was thinking how much easier it would be if he could transform into a jungle cat completely, and get stuck that way and never have to bother with porridge or worry. The porridge was dry and he hated it, but worry was just awful, and try as he might to be a real lion, he could not stop worrying about Marybeth.

CHAPTER 8

Marybeth waited until everyone was asleep, and then she lit the lantern she'd snuck under her blanket and began to read by its light.

She had selected an anthology of personal anecdotes written by people who had experienced their own supernatural occurrences.

She read until her eyelids felt heavy, and then she pinched her cheeks to stay awake. She was afraid to go to sleep, afraid of where she might wander next. She did not want to go back to that farmhouse. Despite the kindness of the old woman, there was something about that place that didn't sit right with her.

She turned the page. "The Odd Occurrence in October" was the title of the next story.

It began on October thirty-first, or as most would call it, Halloween . . .

She read until the words no longer made sense, and then, using the open pages for a pillow, she fell asleep.

That night, a cold wind crept into the house. It breathed its way through the cracks in the windows, and it settled in Marybeth's hair.

She opened her eyes before she fully awoke.

There was something calling her—she sensed it but didn't hear. It had happened earlier that day in the library as well. A pull that tried to make her run away from Lionel and Mrs. Mannerd. She had been able to fight it then, but the gentle suggestion had become violent and pleading.

The blue creature wanted to show her something in the river.

Quietly, she crept down the ladder and past the sleeping older ones.

When she reached the hallway, there was Lionel, curled up and sleeping with a worried expression and a twitch to his leg. He was quite like a mother rabbit, Marybeth thought, so eager to protect its young while all the while knowing the threats of the world were too great to counter alone.

Leave him. It wasn't a voice or even a thought, but rather a pull like the one bringing her to the river.

She walked around him and managed to make it down the steps without making a sound.

She stepped into her boots and buttoned her coat, and opened the door to the chilly autumn night.

"Who are you?" she whispered to the blue creature.

In answer, she found herself standing before the river. This was where it had all started. During the day, the river was gentle and clear. At night it was ink spilled across a page. It was bottomless and looming.

"Why did you bring me here?" Marybeth wasn't sure if she was speaking the words out loud or thinking them. She only knew that the blue creature heard her.

She felt a stirring in her chest as the blue creature breathed in.

And then a blue glow appeared in the river. It was small at first, just like that night when Marybeth fell in and it appeared before her. And just like then, it looked like a fox. Until the water rippled, and the blue light expanded into a human silhouette.

Marybeth edged closer. She felt the water seeping in through the holes in her worn boots, dampening her feet. But the cold and the wet didn't bother her. Her eyes filled with that blue light as she moved closer and closer.

The silhouette looked like her, she thought, with twin braids at either shoulder and a skirt that fanned out below its knees.

The silhouette was saying something, but its voice was lost to the gentle rushing of the water and the wind rattling the dry leaves between the trees, and Marybeth leaned in—

Something pulled her back, and the blue light disappeared and the stirring in her chest turned violent. She was Marybeth and yet not Marybeth at all. She had fangs and claws, and she fought the thing that was trying to hold her.

In some faraway sense, she recognized that the thing that had pulled her away from the water was Lionel. But to the blue creature, he was just a monster. A shadow that had emerged from the woods to harm them. The blue creature pushed him down onto his back and pinned his wrists and snarled.

What the blue creature didn't know, and what Marybeth did, was that Lionel was incredibly brave. There was no fear in his eyes.

"Okay," he cooed. The blue creature had pinned down his wrists but he didn't struggle. He didn't move at all. "Okay, I'm not going to hurt you."

The blue creature was frightened. Marybeth could taste its fear. She could feel it in the marrow of her bones.

"Marybeth." His voice was cool and even and soft. "Are you in there?"

The blue creature had taken over her skin, and Marybeth was nothing but her thoughts. But at the sound of Lionel's voice she found a way to fight back. She forced herself back into her arms and legs, until she could feel Lionel's wrists under her palms, and his hips under her knees.

The blue creature recoiled in fear, and curled up in her chest and went still.

He knew the moment that she had come back. She saw the relief and the hope on his face. "Marybeth?"

She climbed off him and looked over her shoulder, at the river that had gone black and ordinary again. "Did you see it?" she asked.

He sat up, dead leaves clinging to his wild hair. "See what?"

"The blue creature in the water." She looked at him. "It was human. A ghost. I'm sure that's what it was." Her lip had started to tremble, and the rest of her body followed suit. Her body felt weak and weary.

Lionel pulled her collar up around her ears to keep her warm.

"How did you find me?" she whispered.

He smiled. She loved it when he smiled; it made him look like a boy, and he only did it for her. "I can find anything," he said. "Even a blue creature, and even you."

Marybeth took a deep breath and tried to stop shaking. "It's a ghost," she said. "I saw it in the water. I don't know what it wants, I—"

Her voice cracked.

Lionel pulled her to her feet. "Don't worry," he said. "We'll find out what it wants."

Marybeth wanted to ask him how he was so confident. But she said nothing as they walked back to the little red house. For now, she wanted to believe that he was right.

In the morning, Marybeth could barely stay awake as she ate her porridge. She nearly fell asleep midchew.

Despite her slow pace, none of the older ones tried to snatch away her food. Not after what had happened when the hyena boy took her toast. In fact, the children avoided her altogether. They didn't tease her or shove her on the staircase, or call her a runt. They didn't know about the blue creature under her skin, but they could see that something had changed, and it made them nervous.

Marybeth didn't mind being ignored by the older ones. It was a relief more than anything.

She stared sleepily at her breakfast. She could hear Lionel crawling about under the table, gnawing on toast crusts that crunched when he bit into them. After the breakfast plates had been cleared off and the older ones began to get ready for school, Marybeth crawled under the table to join him.

Lionel stopped purring when he saw the bags under her eyes.

"Listen," Marybeth whispered. "After we came back inside, I was up all night reading, and I've found something interesting."

He twitched his nose. He was a rabbit this morning, listening for danger, and this table was their warren.

"The night that I fell into the river and saw the blue creature was October thirty-first," Marybeth said. "Halloween."

Lionel and Marybeth knew a little about Halloween. They knew that some children would dress up like ghosts and goblins and ask their neighbors for treats. Mrs. Mannerd didn't allow it. She had enough on her plate, she said, without having to stitch together eight costumes and pay the dentist when all those sweets rotted the teeth out of their heads.

"The book says that Halloween is the one night of the year when the dead can come back to life. And that's the first time we saw the blue creature, isn't it? On Halloween."

Lionel was skeptical. Until last night he had been sure that the blue creature had been an animal, maybe even a

fox. But Marybeth was right: a fox couldn't climb under her skin.

"The book said that the ghosts don't know they're dead until they're shown."

"How do you show a dead thing that it's dead?" Lionel asked.

"The man had a spirit that would wander his house every Halloween, and one year, he lured it to a graveyard and showed it to its headstone."

Lionel hoped it could be as simple as that. "There's a graveyard just before we reach town," he said.

"I've been thinking," Marybeth said. "If we behave very well this week, and you don't growl and I don't wander off, by Saturday Mrs. Mannerd will trust us by ourselves again. We'll tell her that we're walking into town to return our library books. But along the way, we can stop by the graveyard. If it is a ghost, maybe we can convince it that it's dead, and it will go back to where it belongs."

Lionel hoped for Marybeth's sake that she was right. But whether it was a ghost or not, the blue creature still behaved like an animal, and Lionel would do his best to tame it. At least until Saturday, so that Mrs. Mannerd would let them walk to the library.

All week, the quiet made Mrs. Mannerd nervous. The older ones quarreled and quibbled as usual, but Marybeth and Lionel were eerily demure. Sometimes Lionel would bare his teeth at the other children when they came too close, but Marybeth would whisper to him and he would be a boy again.

But as difficult as it was for Lionel to behave like a human (and a civilized one at that), it was becoming even more difficult for Marybeth to hide the blue creature.

Nobody in the house paid Marybeth much mind, and so they didn't see the way her pupils dilated when a gust of autumn wind rattled the walls. They didn't notice when she darted under the stairs to hide when the paperboy rang the doorbell to collect on the bill.

The nights were always the true challenge, though. After everyone else had gone to sleep, Lionel curled up outside her door, so that she would step on him if she tried to wander off.

As long as Lionel was outside the door, Marybeth did not wander, though. She heard his gentle raspy breathing as he slept, and the blue creature heard it, too, and seemed to be calmed by it.

But while her body didn't wander, her mind did. She had dreams of a little boy she'd never met. In her dreams, he led her to peculiar places. Sometimes it was a well. Sometimes it was a cave, or a river, or a cliff. "Look," he

would say. "There's something that I want to show you."
But something was warning her not to trust him. The
heart beside her own would beat faster, and she would
wake up in a panic. After she awoke, when she tried to
remember the boy's face, all she saw was a blue button
face without eyes.

By Saturday morning, Mrs. Mannerd was very suspi-
cious, especially at breakfast, when Lionel ate his porridge
with a spoon rather than lapping it up with his tongue.

After the bowls had been cleared, Lionel and Marybeth remained at the table with perfect posture and their
hands clasped together.

"Well?" Mrs. Mannerd said. "Aren't you going to go
outside and play?"

Marybeth and Lionel exchanged glances.

"Actually," Marybeth said. "We'd like to walk to the
library."

"The library?" Mrs. Mannerd said. "I could have sworn
your books weren't due back until Tuesday."

"We've finished them, and we'd like to check out
something new," Marybeth said.

Mrs. Mannerd hesitated. All week there had been
something strange in Marybeth's demeanor. Sometimes,
in certain lights, Mrs. Mannerd could believe that Marybeth's eyes turned blue. And Lionel had kept very close to
her—much closer than usual. Even as Marybeth sat on

the bottom step and read for hours, Lionel napped curled by her feet. Odd as it was, she didn't want to discourage them. Closeness of that sort was rare enough for people who had families, and rarer still for those who didn't.

Perhaps it was those supernatural books that had frightened them, Mrs. Mannerd had thought. It was the only explanation.

"I suppose the walk would do you some good," Mrs. Mannerd said. "But wear thick socks, and no more scary books. Pick something nice this time, would you?"

"Yes, Mrs. Mannerd," they said together.

Dutifully, they buttoned their wool coats to their chins, pulled on their boots, and left the house with their library books under their arms.

Mrs. Mannerd stood at the storm door and watched them walk down the dirt driveway. Lionel stooped to bite the head off a dandelion. Even on his best behavior, he would always be just a little bit wild.

CHAPTER 9

"Can you feel it now?" Lionel asked. He was talking about the blue creature's heartbeat.

"Yes," Marybeth said. "I couldn't this morning, but it started up when we left the house."

They had been walking up the road for a quarter mile before the graveyard began to show itself in the distance, like a tiny abandoned city that would never again be inhabited.

The heart sank in Marybeth's chest and disappeared. She staggered when she felt it stop. "It's all right," she told it, and walked ahead of Lionel. "Look. See? There's nothing that can hurt you in there."

The older ones would hold their breath when they passed the graveyard. They told Marybeth and Lionel that if they dared to breathe as the car rolled past, the ghosts would come to their beds at night and drag them to an empty grave and bury them alive.

But Marybeth wasn't afraid of the graveyard. Death itself had never startled her. Her clearest memory of her father had taken place in a graveyard. It was a clear memory, much clearer than a photograph or even the oil painting of Mr. and Mrs. Mannerd that hung in the dining room.

She had been three years old, or maybe four. She had been picking the dandelions and buttercups that grew wild in the grass, gathering them in her pocket. Her father asked if he could hold them, and then he placed them on a headstone and told her, "Say hello to your old mom."

"Why's she down there?" Marybeth had asked him.

"You always put people in the ground when they die," he had said. "The soul is much lighter than the skin and bones. You bury them in the dirt so that they don't float away like a balloon. They just sleep peaceful instead."

Though she was nine years old now, and she knew that death was not the same as sleep, she still believed there was truth in what her father had said. Perhaps the blue creature's spirit had floated up from its grave and gotten lost.

Lionel ran to catch up with Marybeth. They were at the graveyard's entrance now. A low stone fence bordered it, with a high rusty gate emblazoned with iron roses.

Marybeth took a deep breath. *Here goes nothing*, she thought.

The graveyard was more than a hundred years old, and the only one in walking distance, so they both hoped this would work. Even if they weren't sure what they were doing exactly.

Lionel reached for her hand, and Marybeth took his. She hadn't hissed at him in days, and Lionel sensed that the blue creature was coming to trust him. And this was a good thing, because at the sight of all those headstones, Marybeth's eyes flashed blue.

Some of the headstones had fallen to ruin, cracked, chipped, and neglected, because anyone who might have visited them had long since died. Others were newer, with fresh flowers tied with ribbon, letters to the dead tucked in the grass.

If the blue spirit's body was buried here, she didn't know where to begin. She didn't know if the blue spirit had died a hundred years ago, or two hundred, or just last month.

She walked slowly through the rows of headstones.

Lionel walked behind her at a cautious distance, and Marybeth could feel a low growl in her throat that she didn't make. The blue creature was still uncertain about Lionel, but it was coming around to him. Still, there was this fear that Marybeth could feel, as though anyone could be a threat. Even a boy with messy hair who sometimes thought he was a coyote, or a monkey, or a fox.

When the panic began to bubble inside her, it started deep in her stomach. Sometimes the fear made her hide when the doorbell rang, or when the older ones got too close.

Marybeth did her best to calm it. She hummed music in her head, or she concentrated hard on the lines of her favorite poems. She told jokes.

Sometimes it worked, and the blue creature went to sleep inside her skin. But sometimes the fear was unlike anything Marybeth had ever known. Worse than being locked in the closet or missing an answer on a test.

"We could try over here," Lionel said.

His voice was far away, as though Marybeth were hearing it from underwater. She shook her head, trying to clear away the water rushing through her ears, but it only got worse.

The gravestones blurred first, and then everything became a blur. The blue creature darted between her bones, trapped in her rib cage like a fish swimming frantically in a bowl. It was trying to push her out of the graveyard. Wrong, it was telling her. This place was all wrong.

In all the frenzy, she could see Lionel's worried face. She knew he was saying something, but she couldn't hear him. All she could hear was a voice in her mind telling her that this place was wrong, wrong, wrong.

She tried to tell the blue creature to be calm. She tried to hum. But it wouldn't listen.

Lionel had crouched low to the ground, and he approached cautiously. The blue creature snarled.

It took over her legs, and she ran from the graveyard, only distantly aware of the road beneath her feet, her breathing hard, her lungs aching. The worst part about this surge of panic was that it dulled her senses. She had no control of her arms and legs, and everything appeared as though underwater.

From somewhere very far away, she heard Lionel cry out, and she saw the car coming toward her, and felt something swoop her out of the way.

"Hey there," an unfamiliar voice said. "You've gotta be more careful."

Marybeth, her eyes glowing blue, scrambled behind Lionel.

And at last, feeling safe, the blue creature subsided.

When her vision came into focus, she saw a man standing at the edge of the road. His face and clothes were smeared with dirt.

"The road's no place to be running around like a chicken with its head cut off," the man said.

Lionel was finding it difficult to act like a human. He wanted to growl or hiss, to protect both Marybeth and her secret.

It was Marybeth who spoke first. "Yes, sorry, we'll try to be more careful."

Lionel was grateful that at least she knew how to talk to people. That even with this blue creature and its erratic behavior, she could still convince adults that they were just two normal children playing where they ought not to have been.

"Isn't your mother nearby?" the man asked. Now that Marybeth could see him clearly, there was nothing intimidating about him. He hardly looked much bigger than some of the older ones. "Does she know you're playing around outside a graveyard?"

Lionel bit back a growl. The only things more unnerving than people were people that asked questions.

"She isn't here," Marybeth said. "We didn't come here to play. We were visiting a grave."

"Go on, then," the man said. "But be calm about it. Just because these folks are dead doesn't mean they don't deserve respect."

"Yes, sir," Marybeth said. She nudged Lionel, and he echoed an uncomfortable "Yes, sir" of his own.

They turned back into the graveyard, and Lionel whispered, "Did it go to sleep?"

"No," Marybeth said. "I can still feel it. Like goose bumps, but on my bones."

Lionel was quite angry with the blue creature. It could have killed Marybeth, and more than ever he wanted it gone. He had never been so infuriated by a creature in all his life.

But even so, the blue creature had hidden behind him for sanctuary, and that was progress.

Marybeth stopped walking. She squeezed her eyes shut and balled her fists, and whispered, "Be calm, you silly thing."

"What is it?" Lionel asked. He was getting much better at managing conversations, he thought.

"It doesn't like it here," Marybeth said. "I don't know how to explain it. It just feels . . . wrong. All wrong."

She looked as though she wanted to cry, but she didn't. She walked to the gate and picked up the library books where they'd left them and said, "Let's go."

Lionel followed her. "Go where? Is it telling you something?"

"It doesn't matter. I'm done listening to it today," Marybeth said. "Let's just return the books and go home."

After they returned from the graveyard, Marybeth was subdued. Lionel invited her with him to feed the squirrels, but she went to her room and closed the door instead.

At dinner that night, when Mrs. Mannerd laid out the serving dishes, Marybeth didn't even put any food on her plate. She just sat there, staring at the empty white plate with tired eyes. No one noticed, of course. They never did. No one except for Lionel.

And no one but Lionel saw the way she went up the stairs after the dishes had been cleared. Slowly, and against the railing as the older ones ran past her.

After she had brushed her teeth and washed her face, Lionel was waiting for her in the hallway.

"Is it you in there?" he asked.

"Yes, it's me," she said, and to Lionel's great relief he knew she was telling the truth. She lowered her voice to a whisper. "But I don't know for how much longer."

She hugged her arms across her chest. A few weeks ago, Lionel might have compared her to a hatchling whose mother would never return to the nest, leaving her to fend for herself against the predators that lurked when the stars dotted the evening sky. But there was something different to her now. Though she looked the part of a hatchling, when the shadows loomed around her under the darkened sky, she would not be their prey.

She would be a predator.

CHAPTER 10

When Marybeth climbed down from her bunk bed early Monday morning, she was quite awake.

It had taken more than an hour, but she'd gotten the blue creature to feel calm inside her skin. She hummed to it, a melody that she'd heard the late Ms. Gillingham, Mrs. Mannerd's spinster sister, hum as she tended to things around the house. Perhaps it belonged to a song she had heard, or perhaps she had made it up. But Marybeth had always liked it. It seemed, to her, the sort of melody that would fill a nursery's walls as a mother lulled her baby to sleep.

The blue creature had liked it as well. It was fond of Marybeth. Somehow she knew that. It enjoyed soft voices and gentle melodies. Perhaps that was why it had taken to her. There was no other soul so patient and soothing as Marybeth in that red house.

But fond of her or not, the blue creature had to go. Marybeth did not enjoy hissing at the mailman or running out into traffic when the creature was spooked. But worse than that were the dreams. Strange, haunting visions of a boy with a face made from a mosaic of blue buttons, and an ache in her chest, and a terrible sense of grief.

The blue creature made Marybeth know things that she didn't understand. This morning, she knew that the blue creature had left something in the barn of the old farmhouse. Something important.

Maybe, Marybeth thought, she could retrieve it and the blue creature would move on.

She also knew that the blue creature was wary of Lionel, and that if he came along, the blue creature might attack him, or refuse to search for whatever it was it wanted in that barn.

When she opened the bedroom door, she could just barely see Lionel asleep by the threshold. He was there every night to make sure she didn't wander off. Mrs. Mannerd had given up and stopped pestering him about it, and Lionel didn't seem to mind that he got kicked and tripped over when someone got up for a late-night glass of water or to use the toilet.

And his presence there on the floor had helped. Marybeth had not wandered off against her own accord in some time.

This time, it was her own decision to go.

Carefully, she stepped over Lionel's sleeping body. He growled at something in his dream and scratched at his ear. Marybeth waited until he was totally still and quiet, and then she moved down the stairs.

She did feel guilty for going without him. But when anyone was around her, the blue creature was on high alert. Only when Marybeth was alone with it did she have a chance at soothing it.

Sometimes she was able to hum the blue creature to sleep, but for now she was merely trying to keep it calm. She wanted it to show her whatever was in that barn, but she did not want it to take over her body. It was a fragile dance she was slowly learning.

She hummed in her head as she buttoned her coat, and as she pulled on her boots, and wriggled her fingers into her tattered gloves.

It was November now, and Marybeth had vowed to be rid of the blue creature before the first snowfall. The little red house was at the end of a long dirt driveway, at the bottom of a hill. When it snowed, they were stranded there for days. Marybeth suspected the confinement would cause the blue creature to panic, and there wouldn't be a thing she could do to console it, trapped in a house with seven other children.

By the time the farmhouse appeared in the distance, the sun had begun to rise.

"Stay down," Marybeth said, as the blue creature fussed about inside her. It was itching to take over. Marybeth understood. After the blue creature sent her running from the graveyard, she knew what it was trying to tell her. It didn't belong there. It belonged here. "If you go about panicking, I'll walk us back home and we'll never get you sorted out," she warned. "So behave."

She was bluffing, but it worked. The blue creature could tell her what to think and where to go sometimes, but it could never read her mind.

It was her own heart thudding in her chest as she stepped off the road and onto the large yard in front of the farmhouse.

She took a step toward the barn, which always called to her when she was here, but a sound stopped her.

It was coming from the trees, a loud *whack*. Followed by another, and another.

Slowly, she moved toward the sound, clenching and unclenching her gloved fingers to keep them warm. The chilly air was biting at her nose and cheeks.

Whack!

Whack!

Whack!

Not far into the woods, just beyond the tree line, there was a man in a plaid flannel shirt, loading logs onto a stump and chopping them into firewood.

Marybeth recognized him as the old woman's son, Reginald.

His back was to her, and he froze with the ax over his head as though he sensed her standing there.

"What do you want?" he said. "Why do you keep coming back here?"

"I don't know," Marybeth answered honestly.

Reginald set down the ax and turned to face her.

The blue creature ebbed inside her arms and coiled around her heart, trying to take over.

Marybeth clenched her fists. *Be still*, she told it. Her temples ached from the strain of trying to maintain control. Her entire body ached at times, and she empathized now with the grunts and groans that came from Mrs. Mannerd when she stooped to pick up something she had dropped or struggled up the stairs with the final load of laundry. Marybeth felt that she also had the body of an old woman, more and more as the days went on. She was forgetting what it was like to be a young girl, and to run outside and play.

Reginald's breath was a cloud in the cold air. His cheeks were flush and red from the work of chopping so much firewood. He wiped the beads of sweat from his forehead and said, "You walked all this way?"

"It wasn't very far," Marybeth said.

"That orphanage? It's two miles at least." He folded his arms. "What do they do to you there? Beat you?"

"No," Marybeth said.

"Starve you? Lock you in your bedroom?"

"No."

"What then?"

Reginald was tall and slender, with gray streaking some of his dark hair. He was not as old as Mrs. Mannerd, but maybe old enough to be someone's father, Marybeth thought. And though he appeared perfectly normal, Marybeth was unsure whether she should trust him.

"I just like it here."

The man canted his head as he looked at her, as though she were some sort of strange creature that had crawled up through the frost-covered dirt.

The way he looked at her caused the blue creature to turn in her chest. It was trying to wriggle itself into her arms and legs—she could feel it. She balled her fists and clenched her jaw. *Be still*, she told it, *or I am taking us back home.*

Marybeth worried that he would sense the blue creature that was at that very moment fighting with her. She swallowed a snarl in her throat and pushed her fists into her pockets.

"Did you live on a farm with your parents?" Reginald asked. "Is that it?"

Marybeth shrugged. She would have liked to say, "I don't know," which was the truth. She didn't remember where she had lived before she came to Mrs. Mannerd. But her tongue was shaking inside her mouth, because the blue creature was trying to scream.

She clenched her jaw. *Quiet, you foolish thing. I'm trying to help you.*

"You're not much," Reginald said. "I don't suppose you're any good at chopping firewood."

Marybeth watched him pick up the ax. They had one at the red house, kept jammed in a stump by the shed where Mr. Mannerd had kept his tools and things. The two oldest children did all the chopping. Lionel had tried once, and Mrs. Mannerd threatened that if he tried again, he could say good-bye to all his bird feeders and his bringing berries to the foxes because he wouldn't be setting foot outside again until he was a very old man.

"I've never tried," Marybeth said, her voice emboldened by the force of overcoming the blue creature.

"I knew a girl like you once," he said. "Most girls are afraid of axes and sharp things, but she wasn't. She wasn't afraid of anything." He looked at her, and Marybeth felt, for a moment, that she had known him all her life. Longer than that, even. She felt that she had confided her secrets in him long ago.

She shook her head. "I'm not afraid of many things."

"Well, since you're going to stand there gaping, might as well make yourself useful. Come on and take a shot."

Hesitantly, Marybeth stepped forward. Though the red house was nowhere in sight, she still felt that Mrs. Mannerd would somehow sense that one of her children was this close to a blade and would come running to stop her.

But no one came. There was nothing but a cold breeze that bit at her skin through the holes in her gloves, and the ax being offered.

She took it, and its unexpected heft caused her to stumble forward. Reginald laughed, though not unkindly. "Use both hands," he said. "Here." He set a piece of wood on the stump. "Aim right for the center of it. Carry the weight in your forearms."

Marybeth did her best to hide the effort it took to lift the ax. In the red house, she was not even allowed to use the hammer to hang nails for the Christmas garland.

"What happened to her?" she said. "The girl who wasn't afraid of anything."

Reginald narrowed his eyes at her, and she couldn't tell what he was thinking. "She's still around," he said.

The blue creature was a buzzing in her blood. It was as though a beehive had been set loose inside her skin.

He knows something, Marybeth thought. But how to ask him?

She raised the ax, and then, as she was about to strike with it, hot blood rushed through her arms, and she was overtaken by the blue creature. The last thing she saw was the firewood splinter and break apart under the blade, and then everything blurred and she felt herself falling asleep.

CHAPTER
11

"Honestly, you children," Mrs. Mannerd said, wriggling her arms into her wool coat. If the children's clothing was tattered and old, Mrs. Mannerd's coat was older. She had been a much younger woman when she first acquired it, and much thinner, and by now she had let out the seams more times than was reasonable.

It was after eight o'clock now, and the last of the older ones had left for school. Only Lionel was left, with nothing showing of him but the whites of his eyes as he huddled in the darkness under the stairs.

"Come on, Lionel." Mrs. Mannerd sighed. "I need you to work with me today. Put on your boots, and your coat, and your gloves. Hurry and be quick about it. It looks like it might rain."

Lionel crawled across the living room floor, with his belly close to the creaking boards. He was sniffing for traces of Marybeth, who had gone missing the night before. All he knew for certain was that she had taken her coat and her gloves, and thought to close the door behind her. These were not actions of the wild blue creature that had invaded her, but rather they were the actions of the sensible girl he had always known, who braided her hair and said "please" and "thank you."

Had she left on her own? Without waking him?

After he had gotten dressed, Mrs. Mannerd draped a scarf over his shoulders and wrapped it over his ears and chin to keep out the cold.

He followed her to the Cadillac like a lone gosling. He said nothing as he watched Mrs. Mannerd struggle with the engine, muttering curses and prayers in the same breath to make it work.

She hit the steering wheel with a cry of frustration, and for the first time Lionel began to believe that she needed Marybeth as much as he did. In that little red house with its leaky ceilings and its eight children and its pipes that froze when it snowed, Marybeth was predictable, punctual, always reliable. Without her good behavior, their entire world seemed to be in chaos. It was as though there was no goodness in the world at all.

The engine finally started, and Mrs. Mannerd cleared

her throat with the same sort of rusty sound and sat back to wait for the car to warm up.

Lionel hugged his knees to his chest and tried to make himself small. He did not like cars, especially when it was too cold outside to roll down the window. He felt like a bird in a swinging cage, whose wings still worked but who could not fly.

Finally he said, "Are we going to look for her at the farm?"

Mrs. Mannerd looked relieved and impressed that he had spoken. Without being asked a question, no less. "Can you think of any other place she might be?"

"No." Lionel squeezed his knees to his chest. "She's probably there."

He wasn't fretting about where Marybeth would be, but rather who she would be when they found her.

He once thought that he would enjoy it if Marybeth could be wild the way that he was wild. If she growled and burrowed and learned to charm the animals the way that he did, he might not have felt so alone in his strangeness. But with the arrival of the blue creature, the wildness was consuming her, like a snake had opened its mouth and was swallowing her whole. And he wanted her back the way she was, with her spectacles and her kind eyes. He wanted to look up from the grass and find her standing over him, hugging a book in her arms, asking him what he was up to today. Even if they didn't have very much in common, he liked her that way.

The old Cadillac hit every bump in the road, and when the farmhouse appeared in the distance, Lionel felt his stomach go weightless with dread. The car came to a stop, and Mrs. Mannerd turned to him. "Are you coming with me or staying here?"

In answer, he opened his door and stepped outside.

Mrs. Mannerd was thankful for his agreeable behavior this morning. With the way Marybeth was carrying on these days, the old woman in the farmhouse probably thought that the orphanage was a certified zoo.

They walked to the front door, and even before Mrs. Mannerd knocked, Lionel could smell the toast, eggs, and hot tea. He sniffed the air and could smell hot chocolate, too. Ever since the arrival of the blue creature, Marybeth went through fits wherein she could not seem to eat enough. Other days, she hardly ate at all, and Lionel had begun to suspect that this weakened the blue creature and caused it to sleep.

The door swung open, and there stood the old woman in her robe, looking cheerful as ever. "I suspected you'd be along soon," she told Mrs. Mannerd. "Come in, come in!"

Lionel moved past them, through the living room and past the china cabinet that shook when anyone walked by it, and to the kitchen where Marybeth sat at the table eating a pile of eggs and bacon. The old Marybeth ate very little in the mornings, and had never much cared for eggs. But the blue creature made her ravenous as it used up all her body's energy.

He approached her with caution, with his arms at his sides, giving weight to his footsteps so as to announce his presence.

There was nobody in the kitchen with Marybeth, but an empty plate and rumpled napkin suggested that someone had been sitting next to her.

"Marybeth?" he said.

She looked at him, and Lionel was not sure whether it was really her. It was becoming harder to tell.

Though her eyes remained their usual color this time, there were dark bags under them, as though she were a sketch of herself, with her eyes traced over and over again with pencil.

She picked up a piece of bacon and bit into it.

Maybe this wasn't too strange of her, Lionel told himself. Something like bacon was a rare thing back in the red house, and with six other children, neither Lionel nor Marybeth stood much chance of getting a piece to share between them. He couldn't blame her if the sight of it made her greedy.

Lionel was so focused on Marybeth's worn face, trying

to determine whether or not it was her, that the sudden noise outside startled him and he flinched.

He wanted to scramble under the table. But he couldn't turn into an animal here. Not with the blue creature trying to steal Marybeth away. At least one of them had to be a human now.

When the noise came again, he recognized that it was only the sound of firewood being chopped. There was nothing to be afraid of. But he didn't miss the glare Marybeth gave in the direction of the sound, as though she hated it and couldn't bear to go on listening to it.

"Mrs. Mannerd has come to take us home," Lionel said, speaking in the cautious measured tone he reserved for the coyotes.

He held out his hand, and Marybeth stared at it and then at him.

"Come on, children," Mrs. Mannerd called from the end of the hall. "Let's go home. We've imposed enough."

Marybeth didn't move. She shuddered, and only Lionel saw it. One of her feet dragged across the floor, as though she were trying to stand.

"*Marybeth*," Mrs. Mannerd called, exasperated now. She was at least accustomed to Lionel being uncooperative and bizarre, but for once he was perfectly reasonable. Marybeth was the one Mrs. Mannerd didn't know what to do with.

Mrs. Mannerd stomped down the hall. She was the animal now, Lionel thought. A jungle cat moving too fast for him to stop. Lionel tried to warn her, tried to say, "Stop." But it was too late. Mrs. Mannerd grabbed Marybeth by the coat sleeve, and the fragile balance was broken.

Marybeth let out a scream that was not at all human. It was the cry of prey being eaten alive. The sound dug through Lionel's skin and blood, and it hit his bones and made him shiver.

Mrs. Mannerd was barely able to gasp before Marybeth had darted from the room, just a blur of brown tangled hair.

The old woman tried to close the door before Marybeth could escape, but Marybeth was too fast for her. She ran out into the cold morning air and let the screen door slam behind her.

Lionel took a step, and Mrs. Mannerd grabbed him by the collar of his coat. She was not trying to restrain him, Lionel realized. She was trying to protect him. Even Mrs. Mannerd was afraid of what Marybeth was becoming.

Lionel did not struggle. He did not try to break free. He did not scream. He took a deep breath and tried to remember how to be a human boy.

He turned to face Mrs. Mannerd. "Please," he said. "I can find her. She'll listen to me."

It wasn't a lie. While Lionel could not claim to understand the blue creature that was fighting Marybeth for dominance, he did know that Marybeth was in there somewhere.

Mrs. Mannerd stared at him a good long while. Lionel had been in her charge for years, and with each year he'd grown wilder than the last. But in recent weeks she had come to see his reasonable side. He was even polite. She was beginning to realize that for each time Lionel behaved like a cat or a wolf or a monkey, even she had forgotten that he truly was a boy under all of that. And now she could see it clearly.

"Oh, Lionel." She sat in one of the kitchen chairs so that she could meet his eye level. "You're frightened, aren't you?"

Lionel didn't answer, but he didn't have to.

"I don't know what has come over Marybeth," Mrs. Mannerd said. "But I think that she is beyond being able to listen. We can't help her, you and I."

"I can," Lionel said eagerly. "Please." He hated that word. Only humans would ever ask permission. Every other animal in the world knew when it was time to act.

"She isn't well," Mrs. Mannerd said, and there were tears in her eyes. "You see it, I know you do."

She was a mourning mother bird again, but also, strangely, a human. Lionel could see the sadness and the worry in her creased face. He understood. They weren't as different as he'd once thought, and it frightened him.

He turned for the door.

"Wait," Mrs. Mannerd said.

"I can find her," Lionel said. And Mrs. Mannerd didn't try to stop him, perhaps because he had bothered to explain what he was doing.

He ran past the sounds of firewood being chopped and made his way to the barn, where he did indeed find Marybeth. She was huddled behind some hay bales, clawing frantically at the ground.

It was cold in here, and for once Lionel could truly feel it, even through his wool coat.

Marybeth was breathing fast as she dug, and little cold clouds were coming out of her mouth and disappearing. Marybeth was as fragile as those little clouds she breathed. There one moment and not the next.

Lionel knelt beside her. The gloves Marybeth wore were already old and fraying, but now they were coming completely apart. Her fingertips were starting to bleed.

Lionel thought about the claws it would take for an animal to dig through this hard, cold dirt, and he thought about Marybeth's soft touch and gentle hands, and he was quite fed up with this blue creature.

"Listen to me," he said, quite firmly.

The digging stopped. Marybeth looked at him, her dark eyes flickering with bits of blue, as though someone was shining a blue light in them.

"This nonsense has got to stop," he said, recycling what Mrs. Mannerd had told him hundreds of times. "I know you don't mean to be bad. You're just spooked. But there's a way of going about things. If you want help, you have to try to be reasonable. You have to try."

Marybeth's breathing slowed. Her nostrils flared as though picking up Lionel's scent.

"Marybeth will help you," Lionel went on, still speaking firmly. The more he spoke, the easier it became. Even if he did prefer to howl and hiss. "She'd help anyone who asked for it. But you need to free her so she can do it. If you carry on this way, you're going to hurt her, and then where will you be?"

After he had said all he had to say, Lionel sat back on his heels and waited. He did not know if his words would reach the blue creature. He rarely spoke to his animals, and even when he did, it was mostly just nonsense meant to soothe them. They understood tones and gestures, not the words themselves.

But the blue creature inside Marybeth was not like any of those animals.

The blue light left Marybeth's eyes, and all at once she started to shiver in the cold.

She looked at Lionel with that face he had known for most of his life. Just a touch crazed and startled, but familiar.

For once, she was the one who didn't have words. Instead, she crawled to him across the hay and put her arms around him.

Lionel held her and petted her tangled hair and said, "It's all right."

Mrs. Mannerd had followed Lionel to the barn, and now she stood in the doorway, watching them.

She saw the way the children clung to each other. For just the moment, she didn't interrupt them.

Eventually, Marybeth got to her feet, and Lionel kept close to her side as they walked for the car.

Marybeth felt hollow, as though the blue creature had dug a hole for itself in her belly and removed all her organs to make room. Her legs were rubbery, her fingers sore. "Get in the car where it's warm," Mrs. Mannerd said. "Goodness, Marybeth, your skin is turning blue."

Lionel and Marybeth climbed into the backseat. Mrs. Mannerd closed the door behind them, and as she walked around to the driver's side, Marybeth nudged Lionel. "You see that man over there carrying the firewood?"

Lionel followed her gaze to the old woman's son, Reginald, piling the firewood beside the house. He nodded.

Marybeth looked at Lionel, her eyes wide. "He knows something."

Lionel looked hopeful. "What does he know?"

"I'm not sure. I— Maybe he knew the blue creature when it was alive." She hesitated and then put her hand on the door to open it. "I should try again to ask him. I was going to earlier, but then I lost control."

"No." Lionel held the door closed. The sudden worry in his eyes gave Marybeth a chill. "No," he said again. "What if he's the one who killed it?"

CHAPTER 12

Lionel hid in the shadows outside the living room, watching as the doctor opened his suitcase.

Marybeth sat on the couch with a thermometer in her mouth as Mrs. Mannerd paced and fretted before her.

Marybeth did not look at all sick. In fact, she'd made an effort to appear normal. She'd brushed her hair and even braided it. She wore a green gingham dress that was free of any wrinkles or stains, despite being secondhand, and white socks whose holes she had sewn shut and whose lace trim she had repaired.

Only Lionel knew Marybeth's face well enough to see that lines were beginning to form under her eyes. They were very faint and tinged with blue.

She glanced across the room and spotted Lionel in the shadows, and she tried to give him a reassuring smile around the thermometer.

Lionel did not like doctors. He had learned to be like a cat and hide his illnesses when they came so as to avoid the tonics and the pills, but especially the needles. Maybe the only things Lionel hated more than doctors were needles.

As for Marybeth, she had always enjoyed doctors. She enjoyed eating vegetables and brushing her teeth and scrubbing her face until it was pink, making sure her spectacles were straight, her hair combed and clean. She enjoyed being told that she was healthy as a horse—which she always was. She even enjoyed the needles, because the liquid left the syringe and went into her blood to keep her well. She was like a house that cleaned itself, Mrs. Mannerd liked to say.

The doctor was tall and thin, with a complexion almost as gray as his hair. He was very old. Older than Mrs. Mannerd. But he was the only doctor in town who still made house calls, and he never charged Mrs. Mannerd full price for his visits, because he said that she did a noble thing caring for so many children as she did.

The doctor took the thermometer from Marybeth, looked at it, and said, "A perfect ninety-eight point six."

Marybeth sat up a little straighter, proud of herself if only for the meager achievement of passing this test.

Lionel cowered from a distance. He had promised to stay nearby, in case the blue creature returned and he needed to help tame it. But he would not get any closer than this.

The doctor reached into his suitcase and unfolded a footstool. With a grunt and the creaking of bones, he knelt before Marybeth and shined his flashlight down her throat. He checked her reflexes, even looked in her ears. One after another, she passed each of his tests.

But then Lionel saw it. The doctor had outstayed the blue creature's tolerance. He had prodded at her one too many times. Lionel knew this when Marybeth gripped her skirt in her fist. Her chest stopped moving as she held her breath, and her face was determined. She crossed her legs, which were shaking from the strain of trying to stay in control.

Lionel swallowed his fear of the doctor and crawled out from the shadows. He hoped his presence would calm the blue creature, but he was just a second too late.

The blue creature returned with that vicious, protective snarl, followed by a hiss. The doctor nearly toppled off his stool, no doubt startled that such a sweet and small thing as Marybeth could make that fearsome sound. She lashed out, and Lionel could hear her nails raking across the doctor's face.

Mercifully, the blue creature did not attack again, but scrambled across the room on all fours and hid behind Lionel's legs.

Just like that, Lionel forgot the doctor and Mrs. Mannerd. He crouched down before the blue creature, whose eyes were only faintly glowing. "Remember what I told you yesterday," he whispered. "We'll help you, but you have to be reasonable."

The blue creature sat on the floor, and the gesture was almost human. Almost. But the doctor's shadow overtook Marybeth's body and the blue creature whimpered like a frightened animal.

The doctor hunched forward, squinting for a better look. Thin lines of blood were swelling up on his cheek from the scratches.

Instinctively, Lionel stepped in front of Marybeth. He reminded himself not to snarl. That would only make things worse.

Mrs. Mannerd stood beside the doctor, and Lionel saw the hope go out of her face. Marybeth had managed to convince her that she was better, if only for a few moments. "The children are quite protective of each other."

"Yes, yes, I see that," the doctor said. "But in this state, I worry—well—that is—has she harmed any of the children?"

"She wouldn't," Lionel said, and only a moment later realized that this wasn't entirely true.

Mrs. Mannerd covered her eyes with one hand. "A few weeks ago she bit one of the older boys. Three times her size, and she knocked him flat on his back. I wouldn't have believed it if I didn't see for myself."

"She wouldn't hurt me," Lionel insisted.

"Lionel, hush," Mrs. Mannerd said.

"Ah," the doctor said. "I wonder if we might speak privately, then?" With a sweep of his arm, he gestured to the door.

"Yes, of course," Mrs. Mannerd said, and led him into the kitchen.

Just as soon as they were gone, Marybeth covered her eyes. "How bad was it?" she said. "The scratch."

"It was nothing," Lionel said. He was lying, but he didn't care so long as it might console her.

"I nearly killed him," Marybeth said, still covering her eyes.

"It'll barely leave a mark," Lionel said.

Marybeth shook her head. "Not that. Reginald. Back at the farmhouse. He handed me the ax and told me to try chopping the firewood. I knew I wasn't supposed to, but we never get to do anything like that here, and I wanted to try it."

She lowered her hands from her eyes. Her fingers were scarred from all the digging through the hard earth. Even when she looked like herself, parts of the blue creature were taking over her skin.

"As soon as I'd raised the ax, this strength overtook me, and it was like I was watching everything happen in a dream. It tried to make me swing the ax right into his chest. Or—someone's chest. All I know is that the blue creature wanted to do something terrible. I don't know how I managed to stop it, but I was able to drop the ax and run.

"Once I got as far as the farmhouse, the old woman who lives there came out and offered me something to eat. And I think—the blue creature likes her. I'm not sure why. I remember stepping inside, but after that it's all foggy until you found me in the barn."

She hugged her knees to her chest. "Lionel, what am I going to do? I don't want to hurt anyone. Why would it want me to kill Reginald? He was nice."

"Maybe he isn't nice," Lionel said. "Maybe the blue creature sees something that you don't."

Marybeth shook her head. "No," she whispered. "Something made it angry, but it wasn't him. It's got a vicious side, and I'm scared of what it will make me do. It's getting harder to control."

"Don't try to control it," Lionel said. "You can't control wild animals. You can only listen to them. That's how

you'll come to predict its behavior and understand what it wants."

"I can't be like you," Marybeth said. "I've been trying for years. I want to see things the way you see them, but I just can't. I'm too ordinary."

"If you were ordinary, none of this would be happening," Lionel said, and for the first time in weeks, he laughed.

Marybeth forced a smile.

"Anyway, you don't need to see things the same way that I do," he said. "You'll always have me. I'm not going anywhere."

"It does seem to like you," Marybeth said. "For now, at least. But you must be careful. You can't let it hurt you. If it takes over, and it can't be stopped, promise me you'll do whatever you have to do to protect yourself."

This was why Lionel hated using words. He knew what Marybeth was asking, but he couldn't bring himself to promise that he would hurt her if it meant protecting himself against the blue creature's wrath. He wouldn't.

He sat beside her, and she rested her head against his shoulder. Neither of them said anything more.

CHAPTER 13

After the doctor was gone, Mrs. Mannerd set about doing the only thing she knew to do when she was worried.

She cooked.

It would be another hour still before the older children returned from school. And after that mess with the doctor, Marybeth was quiet. She was sitting under the kitchen table reading a book, with Lionel curled beside her like a house cat. It was impossible to know which one of them was trying to comfort the other.

Mrs. Mannerd did not know what was happening to Marybeth, but she blamed herself for whatever it was. It must have been difficult for that bright and well-behaved child to grow up in such chaos, without her own mother to raise her properly. She needed more than this little red house could provide for her, Mrs. Mannerd thought.

The truth was that Marybeth probably could have been adopted years ago. She could be living right now in a house of her own, with parents who doted on and loved her.

When she had first arrived at the little red house, she was a tiny thing with pink chubby cheeks and soulful eyes. She was quiet but warm, undeterred by the tragedies of her young life and inquisitive about everything. She had followed Mrs. Mannerd around the kitchen, watching the way she measured the butter and sifted the flour and cracked the eggs.

By then, the war had been over for more than a decade. Times were especially trying, and most were struggling to take care of their own children, never mind looking to take in any strays. But still, there were a few who had inquired about Marybeth. And Mrs. Mannerd had been unwilling to part with her.

She had her reasons. They seemed too strict, or not strict enough, or they already had a small litter of their own, or they wouldn't have the means to provide for her in the way that she deserved.

But there was another reason, too.

Years before that, when Mrs. Mannerd was a young newlywed, Mr. Mannerd built her that little red house with the hope that they could one day fill the rooms with children of their own.

Only the children never came. Year after year and one doctor after another, there were no explanations as to why.

It was Mrs. Mannerd's sister who suggested that the couple take in a few of the unwanted children. There was certainly no shortage of those.

So, in one way or other, the rooms were filled with children. Something was always cooking on the stove, and there was always water in the tub, and there was always something that needed to be cleaned, and someone to help clean it.

Sometimes a noisy house is the only thing to make up for the emptiness.

Just as children went, children arrived. Tall ones and short ones, clean ones and sloppy ones. Some of them, adults with children of their own now, still wrote letters on the holidays. Others dropped off the face of the earth.

But for all the children who had come and gone through that door, there was only one who ever reminded Mrs. Mannerd of the child she had always longed to have.

Marybeth.

Marybeth herself had no way of knowing this, but she quite resembled Mrs. Mannerd as a child. She had the same sharply parted brown hair, the same nearsighted

vision, and the same shyness. And the way that she could tame that wild boy, Lionel—well, that was some magic.

And she had always seemed happy here. Well adjusted, well groomed, literate, and kind. Mrs. Mannerd had hoped that Marybeth would grow into a happy woman one day, and that at the very least she'd visit sometimes for tea.

But now Marybeth's mind was starting to slip away. If only Mrs. Mannerd had let her be adopted by one of those nice couples, none of this would be happening. She had to fix this somehow.

"Marybeth," she called from the stove.

"Yes, Mrs. Mannerd?" She sounded so much like her normal self that it was a heartbreak.

"Come and mind the soup while I season the roast."

Dutifully, Marybeth dragged the footstool to the stove and stirred the bubbling pot.

Mrs. Mannerd stood beside her as she minced the garlic. "I wanted to speak with you about what happened this afternoon," she said in a low voice.

Marybeth stared guiltily into the pot and nodded.

"You aren't a bad child, Marybeth," Mrs. Mannerd said. "I know that you don't want to run away or hurt people. But sometimes—oh dear, how do I say this? Sometimes there are wires in the brain that just fry up. Like the time I plugged too many things into the extension cord and it blew sparks."

Marybeth started to get a sick feeling in her stomach. Broken. Mrs. Mannerd was trying to tell her that she was broken.

"It isn't as uncommon as one might think," Mrs. Mannerd said, trying to sound cheery. "It's just the sort of thing people don't talk about, that's all."

Marybeth could certainly understand that. She and Lionel had done their best to hide her strange new affliction. If it wasn't all better, there was some peace in pretending that it was.

"It happened to my grandmother, in fact," Mrs. Mannerd said. "One day she forgot how to use a fork and thought that Millard Fillmore was president."

Marybeth didn't know what to do with herself, so she stirred the stew. Finally she asked, "Did your grandmother get better?"

"No, dear. No, she didn't. But she was very old, and you are very young. That makes all the difference. You can bounce right back from this, the same way you bounce back from a cold."

Marybeth dreaded the answer, but still she forced herself to ask, "How?"

Mrs. Mannerd lowered the flame on the stove and put her hand over Marybeth's to stop the stirring.

"The doctor has recommended a place that could help you. It specializes in children with—well—with

difficulties. We have an appointment to see it tomorrow morning."

Marybeth went pale. She did not try to argue or cry. She was too postured for that. Too good. But she wouldn't have minded if the blue creature took over right then and clawed through the screen door so that she could escape.

"You aren't being punished, even if it may seem that way," Mrs. Mannerd said. "This is to make you better."

It wouldn't work. That was what Marybeth wanted to say. She had fallen into a river and a ghost swam inside her, and now it would never leave.

After the silence had become unbearable, Mrs. Mannerd said, "Do you have anything to say?"

Marybeth forced herself to look at her. "Will I be able to come home?"

Mrs. Mannerd drew a deep breath. But if she had an answer, she didn't get to give it before she was interrupted by a crash in the dining room that shook the floor itself.

She ran into the dining room with Marybeth at her heels, and discovered that the china cabinet had been toppled over. Bits of the good dishes and teacups were scattered everywhere, and the front door was open, revealing light flurries of snow and letting in a bitter chill.

"Lionel!" Mrs. Mannerd cried, but he was long gone.

Marybeth found him on the big rock by the river, gnawing on a stick trying to sharpen it.

"Here, I've brought your coat," she said. "Please wear it. I don't want you to get pneumonia."

Lionel stopped chewing only long enough to do as she asked.

"I wouldn't go back to the house for a while," Marybeth said. "I've never seen Mrs. Mannerd so mad. That's the very worst thing you've ever done."

"Good," Lionel said, and spat out a mouthful of splinters. "I want her to send me away, too."

Of course he'd overheard. He heard everything in that house because he knew all the places to listen while still being out of sight.

Marybeth sat next to him. "You know that won't work," she said. "Mrs. Mannerd isn't going to send you away. There's nothing wrong with you."

"There are plenty of things wrong with me," Lionel said.

"Not like there is with me," Marybeth said. "Maybe it won't be such a bad thing. Maybe it will help."

Lionel looked sharply at her. "You don't really think that."

She hugged her arms to her chest. "I don't want to hurt anyone else. Maybe I should be sent away. Maybe it's where I belong."

"Stop it." Lionel stomped his foot against the rock. "Stop it, stop it, stop it! That isn't true."

"Having a tantrum isn't going to solve anything," she said pertly. "You should apologize to Mrs. Mannerd. A lot of those dishes were from France."

"I don't care about France," Lionel muttered into the stick. There were few things in this world he cared about at all, and he was about to lose one of them.

"If you behave—and I know you can, you've been doing so well—I'm sure Mrs. Mannerd will let you come visit me."

Lionel inspected the chewed point of the stick.

"Oh, come now. What are you planning to do with that?" Marybeth said.

"Rip apart the mattresses," he said, feeling ashamed under her scrutiny. She didn't have to say a word. With a grumble he dropped it and watched it roll into the river. That horrible river where all of this had started.

Marybeth crawled to the river's edge and looked inside. But of course it offered no answers. There was no trace of the ghost—it wasn't the river that was being haunted. It was her.

Lionel looked too. "Why did you go back to the farmhouse alone?" he asked. "Why didn't you wake me up?"

"I thought I had a better chance of controlling it if I went by myself," she said. "There's something about that farmhouse. Something about the river and that barn keep pulling me back there. I want to go where the blue creature tells me, so that I can help it. But I'm starting to think it isn't leading me anywhere. It's just doing as it pleases and forcing me along."

Lionel stared hard at the water, and he tried to think of a plan. But all the water did was remind him of his fear that she had been lost forever.

"Promise me you won't go alone again," he said.

"Promise," she said.

Mrs. Mannerd was up all night. She unraveled her nicest sweater and used the yarn to knit a pair of gloves for Marybeth to cover those scratches on her hands. She wanted her to look her best for tomorrow's tour of the institution. She added ruffles to the wrists and tried to assure herself that tomorrow would be for the best.

Upstairs, Marybeth dreamed of the boy with the blue button face and stirred in her sleep.

Meanwhile out in the hallway, Lionel kept guard over Marybeth and the blue creature both. He would not sleep. Tonight, he was the nocturnal owl, lingering up in the trees where he could see all. He was silent and invisible. If anything came out of the darkness that posed a threat, he would swoop.

But the only threat that came was the morning's first light. It meant that soon Marybeth would be gone.

With the light, so also came the sound of the older ones getting out of their beds. Drawers were pulled open. Feet moved across the floorboards. Lionel shrank against the wall and made himself a chameleon as dingy and green as the peeling paper on the walls.

He did such a good job of it that even Marybeth walked past him. He watched her trod down the hallway as though some bird of prey were carrying her in its talons, flying so low that her feet still dragged against the ground.

When he saw her again at the breakfast table, she looked very much like a girl: clean and braided and sitting up straight. She didn't eat. She had to subdue the blue creature. Fortunately, with the way the older ones clambered and fought over each crumb on the table, Marybeth didn't have to resist temptation for very long before there was nothing left to tempt her.

The older ones lined up and followed one another out the door, one after the next. Shoving and giggling and chattering, they didn't look back to see Marybeth still sitting at the table, staring at the empty spot where the plates had been.

They were silly creatures. Lionel had always thought so. They wouldn't notice when Marybeth was gone. They wouldn't notice that the entire world had changed.

Lionel crawled under the table and tugged at the hem of Marybeth's skirt so that she would join him. She was wearing a dress that was an unnatural shade of mint green, both bright and faded at the same time, with a bibbed collar and three white buttons that didn't button anything.

She folded her legs neatly as she settled. She was trying so very hard to be human.

Lionel leaned close to her. "Let's run away," he said.

"Where?" Marybeth asked.

"Somewhere far. Maybe France."

"We'd need a boat," she said.

"No," he said. "We'd lie on our backs on the water and float the whole way. Just us. We could do it."

"And what would we do when we got to France?"

"Live in the wild, where it's just the trees and the animals. We wouldn't have to study a bit; I already know the language."

"Is there a lot of wilderness in France?" Marybeth said, and giggled. But Lionel had been quite serious, and he frowned. He had not done a proper job convincing her, and he opened his mouth to try to say something more persuasive, but he was interrupted when the front door opened.

Lionel's nostrils flared. He always knew their tutor by the perfume she wore, like something sweet that had

been left sitting out for too long and had begun to turn rotten.

"Children?" Mrs. Mannerd called from beside the table. "Where have they gotten off to? They were just here a moment ago."

Marybeth climbed out from under the table and said, "Right here, Mrs. Mannerd."

Lionel felt horribly alone. He forced himself to follow her. "Can't I go along as well, Mrs. Mannerd?" he said, forcing himself to be polite.

"After the damage you did yesterday, you'll be lucky if I let you set foot out of this house again," Mrs. Mannerd said, but she didn't sound mad. Her eyes were dark and she looked tired. "If you behave for your tutor and this house is still standing when I return, we'll talk about letting you have your crumbs for the squirrels again sometime this decade. Marybeth, get your coat." At Lionel's sullen expression, she softened. "I've told you, today is just supposed to be a tour. We'll be back in a few hours."

Marybeth did as she was told. And then Mrs. Mannerd was steering her outside and saying something about new gloves.

Lionel rushed to the window and watched them get into the car. Only it wasn't a car. It was a giant beast with teeth, about to swallow them whole.

Just as Mrs. Mannerd adjusted the mirror and prepared to back down the driveway, Marybeth opened her door. Quick as a blur she ran back to the house. The screen door slammed against its frame, and before Lionel could move, she had thrown her arms around him.

She kissed his cheek.

He was too stunned to move. And by the time he thought to put his arms around her, she was already gone. Through the window he saw her run back to the car.

He had smelled the cold in her hair. He had felt her human heart beating against his chest.

CHAPTER 14

It was a gray morning. The sort of day that felt like the whole earth had gotten caught inside a storm cloud and the rain would be along any minute.

The blue creature was deep asleep, but Marybeth could feel slight reverberations in her chest, as though it was snoring.

You've gotten me into this mess, she thought. They had been in the car for more than an hour, and Marybeth didn't know if she would ever see the little red house again. Mrs. Mannerd had called today a tour, but she had also packed some things for Marybeth in a hatbox. It slid across the backseat every time the car hugged a curve in the road.

Marybeth didn't talk. She was afraid that her voice would wake the blue creature, but she also didn't have anything to say. What could she possibly say?

It had been a while since they'd passed any buildings. The trees were all barren. There were no stores. No other cars. The road was overrun with roots.

Mrs. Mannerd gripped the steering wheel. She was a statue of a woman, Marybeth had always thought. Not sentimental or emotional or easy to rattle. Not like her jittery, chatty sister Ms. Gillingham had been. But even Mrs. Mannerd was starting to come undone because of this blue creature, and she didn't even know that the thing existed.

This drive was for the best, Marybeth told herself. It was best for everyone that she was someplace where she couldn't hurt them. To comfort herself she imagined that there would be a garden at this new place, that she could spend her days outside with the sunlight beating down on the part of her hair.

Mrs. Mannerd fidgeted with the map that was resting on the seat beside her. She glanced at it and then at the road. "It should be the next turn," she said, trying to sound cheerful.

Marybeth gripped her skirt in her fists and willed the blue creature to remain asleep.

The car turned down a road made up mostly of dirt, with some bits of gravel to indicate it had once been cared for. The trees around the road were hunched over, so low that their branches scratched the windows as they drove past.

Mrs. Mannerd cleared her throat.

"Marybeth," she said, "I want you to know that I've always—that is, I care about your well-being, and this isn't a punishment. Do you understand?"

"Yes," Marybeth said. She did understand; Mrs. Mannerd was only doing what adults did. She and Lionel had tried to fix this, and they had failed.

Mrs. Mannerd stopped the car. She didn't bother to pull off to the shoulder. It didn't seem as though anyone else would be coming up the road anyway.

Mrs. Mannerd turned to face her. "Before we go on, isn't there anything you'd like to say?"

"Like what?" Marybeth asked. She was staring at her lap, and she glanced uneasily at Mrs. Mannerd.

"Like about the morning that you were missing," Mrs. Mannerd said. She was trying to be patient, and she said her words slowly. "You walked all that way down the road. You must have been thinking something. And all those other times you wandered off."

Marybeth looked through the windshield. She could not see the building that awaited them farther up the road, but she could sense it. She was so very far away from anything she had ever known, and there could be no turning around. She swallowed a lump in her throat and tried not to cry.

"Marybeth?"

"I don't remember," Marybeth whispered.

"I've had plenty of children who were fibbers," Mrs. Mannerd said. "Enough to tell you that you've never been very good at it."

Marybeth only gripped at her skirt. She did want to tell the truth, but it wouldn't have helped any. There was no adult on earth who would believe her about the blue creature. Probably this place where she was going was filled with people who had secrets they kept to themselves because no one would believe them.

Eventually, Mrs. Mannerd started driving again.

In the little red house, Lionel was getting increasingly restless. For more than an hour he sat at the dining room table, pretending to care about long division as the tutor droned on.

Normally, Mrs. Mannerd would not leave him alone with the tutor. She said that his antics would give the poor woman an ulcer. But today she needed his cooperation, she said, and begged him to behave like a normal

boy. Behaving like a boy meant he had to be treated like one. And today especially, he had more important matters to tend to.

He couldn't very well just run out the door. The tutor would chase after him, and even if she didn't catch him, she would see where he had gone and call the police.

No. He would have to choose stealth over speed.

He forced himself to cough, and then again, and then again.

The tutor set down her pencil, which she had been using to go over his answers, and she felt his forehead. "What's the matter?" she said. "Are you feeling sick?"

Lionel did his best to look pitiful, and he sniffled and coughed again. "Only a little," he said feebly. "My throat is scratchy."

"Oh, dear," the tutor said. "Is there any medicine in the house? Should I call the doctor?"

"Mrs. Mannerd usually makes a cup of tea for us when we cough," Lionel said. "With honey."

The tutor stood. "You just sit right there, then, and I'll be back with some tea."

Lionel forced his sweetest, most innocent of smiles. His cheeks ached, but the tutor didn't notice. She patted his head and walked into the kitchen. "Where does Mrs. Mannerd keep the honey?"

"In the cabinet above the stove," Lionel said, already sneaking for the door. This ought to buy him at least a minute or two; there was no honey in the cabinet. One of the older ones had asked for it and Mrs. Mannerd had said that she was not made of money and then she'd gone into a lecture about the cost of things.

For once, Lionel ran outside without slamming the door behind him. He closed it quietly, and darted behind the hedges that bordered the driveway, so that he could make it to the road without being seen.

In his haste, he had even remembered to grab his coat. He was quite proud of himself for remembering, but he also felt restricted by the weight of that thick wool.

Once he reached the road, he became a jungle cat, covering several yards in a second. He would have to be quicker than a little boy could be.

He didn't know how long it took him to get to the farmhouse. Time no longer mattered. The tutor surely knew that he was gone by now, but that didn't matter because Mrs. Mannerd wouldn't be home for hours.

He snuck past the house and into the barn. It was, after all, the place the blue creature kept returning to. Whatever he was looking for, whatever it would take to save Marybeth, it had to be here.

Along the wall, beside old dingy bales of hay, there were some tools that looked as though they hadn't been used in years, rusty and huddled together, sharing a dress made of cobwebs.

The barn still appeared to be in good condition. Lionel had noticed this before. There was no reason for it to be abandoned, and yet it was. There was something hiding here. Lionel was sure of that. Something the blue creature had tried to use Marybeth to dig up. And now Marybeth was gone, and it was up to him.

He reached through the cobwebs for the shovel.

The building came into view. It was very old. It was made up of stone the color of pale skin, and its windows were murky black eyes. Some crumbling black steps led up to a yawning mouth.

There was no sign. There was only a rusted brass number on the door: 762.

If Lionel were here, he would not allow them to step inside. He would say this building was going to chew them to death in its fangs.

Or maybe, Marybeth thought, she was finally starting to see things the way that he did.

If Mrs. Mannerd had reservations, she didn't let on. She shut off the engine and came around to Marybeth's door and opened it for her. Mrs. Mannerd took Marybeth's hand in one of her own hands and gripped the frayed cord of the hatbox in the other.

Marybeth swallowed her fear, a task that was growing increasingly difficult, and allowed Mrs. Mannerd to lead her up the steps.

It was silent here, and for a hopeful moment, Marybeth thought they had arrived at the wrong place. Taken a wrong turn somewhere and wound up at an abandoned mansion filled with nothing but mice and faded possessions that once belonged to the living.

Mrs. Mannerd knocked on the door, and the sound of those three firm knocks echoed within the building like they were trying to escape.

The blue creature stirred within Marybeth's stomach. It awoke slowly, but once it was conscious, it was strong.

Marybeth stepped back, tried to jerk her hand out of Mrs. Mannerd's, but Mrs. Mannerd was holding on tight.

"Marybeth, what is it?" she said.

Marybeth's eyes were blue, and Mrs. Mannerd blinked several times, sure it was a trick of the light that peeked through the clouds. But Marybeth's eyes stayed blue. Even her cheeks were an odd shade of bluish gray, and the roots of her braids as well, as though some peculiar ink was oozing out of her scalp.

It wasn't just the color of Marybeth's eyes. It was the look in them. Mrs. Mannerd could swear that she was looking at a stranger.

The door swung open.

CHAPTER 15

Lionel dug with more strength than a boy his size ought to possess. His arms were aching, and yet he did not relent.

Time and again, the blue creature had brought Marybeth to this barn, and always it came to rest in the same spot, beneath the hay.

The dirt was hard and nearly frozen, and Lionel's greatest effort brought little result, but still he dug. He knew that whatever the blue creature wanted, it was here. He would find it and bring it to the blue creature, and maybe then it would let Marybeth go. It had to.

Lionel did not know exactly where Mrs. Mannerd was taking Marybeth, but he could imagine. Before he came to the little red house, he had been brought to another place. A darker, colder house filled with broken boys and broken girls. Their bones were intact, but something within them had been damaged. Some of them screamed, or hid under beds, or bit the hands that brought them their dinner.

Lionel knew that he was nothing like them, but he had nowhere else to go. That is, until Ms. Gillingham arrived one bright summer afternoon, holding her purse before her stomach and smelling of perfume. She had a round belly, the roundest Lionel had ever seen, and her smile was big to match it.

She inspected each of the children without flinching, without wrinkling her nose at the smell of them. She said "hello" even if they did not look at her.

Later, Lionel would learn that Ms. Gillingham did this often. She went to homes for broken children and looked for one or two that might be salvaged yet.

Why she chose Lionel was anyone's guess. She'd found him hiding under the kitchen sink, and it was only with infinite patience that she had gotten him to tell her his name. And after he was brought to the little red house, he'd screamed when they tried to put him in the bathtub.

Marybeth was his opposite, Lionel knew. She didn't belong in a home for broken children. She was too good, too hopeful. If Mrs. Mannerd left her in that place, she would die.

It had been nearly an hour now, and he was making some progress with the dirt. He had dug a hole that went past his ankles now. Something was here, and with each jab of the shovel, he braced himself for whatever it was. Surely it was something terrible. Nothing good was ever buried that didn't grow.

Lionel knew a great lot about terrible things, though he never spoke about them. Not even to Marybeth. Especially not to her. He didn't want her to ever know the things he had seen.

The scream was not Marybeth's, though it came from her mouth.

"Please!" Mrs. Mannerd said. She had dropped the hatbox now, and was holding on to Marybeth's wrist with both hands to keep her from escaping.

Marybeth's head shook wildly, and she screamed and screamed in a way Mrs. Mannerd had never seen in all her years minding children. That was how she knew that this rabid creature was no little girl. Something had overtaken Marybeth, and the way she was carrying on, Mrs. Mannerd would have believed it was the devil himself.

Women came running from the open door like a fleet of ghosts. Strong ghosts, who took Marybeth by the arms and legs and carried her inside, all as she thrashed and screamed that awful scream.

With shaking hands, Mrs. Mannerd picked up the hatbox filled with the things she had packed for Marybeth. She fought every instinct to retrieve Marybeth from the nurses who were carrying her away. She was out of sight now, swallowed up by the mint-green hallway that led into the house's belly, but her screams still echoed.

They're going to help her, Mrs. Mannerd told herself. This will be for the best.

"Come on in," a soft voice said, and Mrs. Mannerd looked into the face of an old woman undeterred by the chaos. "I'm Delores. We spoke on the telephone. I've been expecting you both."

Mrs. Mannerd had seen all sorts of places in her lifetime. Happy places and sad places. Some rich places, mostly poor places. She had seen funeral homes and hospitals. But she had never seen a place like this.

The floor was made of old marble tile, and some of the tiles were cracked and chipped. In the entryway there was a wide staircase with a faded yellow carpet that was shredded and frayed.

Delores led Mrs. Mannerd down a long hallway. It had bright peach walls that glowed in the gloomy light. At the end of the hallway was an office with overstuffed leather chairs, so shiny and polished they looked like they were wet. There was also a large desk with nothing on it but a lamp, a pad, and a row of sharpened pencils.

"Please do have a seat," Delores said, as she sat behind her desk. "I'm glad you were able to make it out here. I assume the girl is Mary?"

"Marybeth," Mrs. Mannerd said, and her hands began to tremble at the name. She hadn't known what to expect when she brought Marybeth out here, but she hadn't expected such a fit. "She's normally such a calm girl. She's always been one of my quiet ones."

Delores smiled. She didn't seem to find any of this unsettling, which caused Mrs. Mannerd to wonder if there had been more children like Marybeth. "I assure you, Mrs. Mannerd, I've seen all sorts of tantrums. They do happen. How long has Marybeth been in your charge?"

"Five years," Mrs. Mannerd said. She held the hatbox in her lap.

Delores selected a pencil and reached for her pad. "And what's known about her parents?"

"Not very much, I'm afraid," Mrs. Mannerd said. "Her mother died just after she was born, and her father succumbed to tuberculosis. She has a second cousin in Canada, but she couldn't afford to keep her, and so she found her way to me."

Delores wrote a few notes, but angled the pad so that Mrs. Mannerd wouldn't be able to read.

Mrs. Mannerd's stomach ached with her anxiety. "Can't I go and see her?"

"If you'd like to see her before you leave, you certainly can. But after that we don't encourage visitors for at least a month. It can delay progress. What's in that hatbox?"

"I've brought a few things from home. Extra socks and soap and the like."

Delores's smile never waned. "That won't be necessary. She'll have everything she needs here."

Mrs. Mannerd worried like she had never worried before. Her own instincts were telling her to run down that mint-green hallway and snatch Marybeth away from those nurses and take her home.

But then what? Despite her care and patience, Marybeth had only gotten worse. She had harmed one of the older children. She scratched that doctor. She continued to run away at night. There was no shortage of terrible things that could happen to a small girl out alone in the middle of the night.

She wanted to take her home, but she knew that she couldn't.

After Delores had finished with her questions about Marybeth's health, she led Mrs. Mannerd along.

"Where are the other children?" Mrs. Mannerd asked. It had finally occurred to her how quiet this place was. A home for children, even sick children, should never be quiet.

"In their rooms," Delores said. "I find it's best for them to be separated, so that they don't antagonize one another. Here we are." She reached into the collar of her dress and extracted a necklace that contained several keys. She shuffled through them and found one that opened the door near the end of the hallway. The door was as mint green as the walls, and blended in so well that Mrs. Mannerd almost hadn't seen it.

"This won't be her permanent room," Delores said, working the key into the lock. "All our new patients spend a night or two in here for monitoring, and then she'll be brought upstairs."

Delores opened the door, and for one hopeful moment, Mrs. Mannerd expected Marybeth to run up and hug her and ask to be taken home.

What she saw, instead, was that strange creature she'd seen on the front steps outside. She didn't know how to describe it. It was Marybeth and not Marybeth.

The room had only one window, which was higher than Mrs. Mannerd's head. And it had a single bed with white sheets and a metal frame. There Marybeth was, with her hands and feet tied to all four corners of the

bed, shivering like a rabbit about to face the chopping block.

"Are the restraints really necessary?" Mrs. Mannerd said. Her own voice felt miles away. She thought that she might faint.

"Our methods may seem unnerving at first, but I assure you, they yield results," Delores said. "When our children behave hysterically, this is where they end up. Most get wiser and are never brought here again."

Mrs. Mannerd took a shaky step forward. "Marybeth?"

Marybeth looked at her, and to any stranger, the look on her face might have been taken for anger. But Mrs. Mannerd knew her, and knew that it was something else. This was not the sweet child she had cared for all these years. Mrs. Mannerd could not shake the feeling that this was not Marybeth at all.

She was still wearing her new gloves. Her fingers wriggled helplessly in their restraints, but she had stopped truly fighting.

Mrs. Mannerd knelt by the bed. She tried to pet Marybeth's hair, but a low growl stopped her, and she withdrew her hand.

"This isn't forever," she said. "I'll come and visit. And once you're better, I'll take you back home for good. Do you understand? This isn't permanent."

Marybeth's lips parted, and it looked as though she wanted to say something. There was a moment of recognition in her eyes.

But all that came out of her was a growl and then a whimper, like a fox that had its leg caught in a trap.

During the long drive back to the little red house, the hatbox sat in the seat where Marybeth had been just an hour before, and Mrs. Mannerd could not remember the last time that she had been so sad.

CHAPTER 16

The shovel hit something hard, and at last Lionel allowed himself to stop digging. Despite the cold air, his face was sweating and his shoulders felt like they were on fire.

The hole he dug went past his waist now, and he knelt in the loosened dirt and began to brush it away.

There was something buried here, and now he could sense it, the way animals sensed rain. He dug through clumps of dirt, pebbles, and frail broken roots.

His fingers touched the hard thing that he'd first struck with the shovel. But when he brushed more of the dirt away, the first thing he saw was the color yellow.

At least, he thought it must have once been yellow. The fabric was filthy and so faded that he could almost see right through it.

In his confusion, he wondered if the blue creature had buried it here. That it might have been an old doll from the little red house that hadn't been played with since Marybeth lost her interest in toys.

But the more dirt he cleared away, the longer the yellow fabric proved to be, until it was much too long for a doll, but just the right size for a real human girl.

He reached the hem of the fabric, scalloped with dirty white lace, and a small black shoe with a leather bow.

His heart was beating so loud by then that he felt it in his ears. Attached to the shoe was a solid white bone. The yellow dress was filled with bones as well.

Lionel stopped. He closed his eyes and tried, tried, tried to think of what the foxes or the birds would do. He tried to be any animal that came to his mind. An elephant or a tiger or the sparrows like the ones on the kitchen curtains.

But his mind would not let him. He was human, only human, and he couldn't stand it.

He sat on the ground for a very long time before he had the courage to clear away more of the dirt. All his animal instincts had abandoned him by then, and he saw through his human eyes.

There were legs, ribs, arms, fingers, lying fragile in the dirt, like a puzzle that would come apart if he disturbed the pieces.

And then, right where it should be, there was a skull. All together, the pieces made up a girl, about the same size as Lionel. Or, he thought, the same size as Marybeth.

"It's you," he said to the empty spaces where its eyes should be. This was why the blue creature had run away when they stepped into the graveyard. This was why it kept leading Marybeth back to this barn in the middle of the night. It was trying to find its body, and it knew it would be here.

The blue creature had been human all along.

"I'll come back," Lionel said. He began to lay the dirt back in place, so that nobody else would uncover what he'd found. "I won't leave you here forever. I promise." But he knew there was no one to hear him. He was only talking to bones and cloth. The blue creature was not here. It was with Marybeth, who had been taken away. He would have to find her and bring her here.

Lionel arrived at the little red house just seconds before Mrs. Mannerd. She saw him darting out from between the shrubs. He saw her, too, and realized that he'd been caught. But worse, he saw that the passenger seat was empty.

Mrs. Mannerd got out of the car. She looked tired, and Lionel could sense her sadness even from several yards away. "Oh, Lionel, what have you been up to now?" she said, exasperated.

"Where's Marybeth?" he said.

"Lionel—"

"You said you wouldn't leave her. You said you wouldn't!"

He ran for the road, but this one time Mrs. Mannerd was faster than he was. She had lost a child today, and she wasn't about to lose another. She grabbed his arm and pulled him back.

"Lionel, listen to me." She knelt to his level and gripped his shoulders. "Marybeth is sick. She's very sick. She's going to get what she needs there."

Lionel squirmed angrily but could not free himself from her grasp. "She needs me," he said. "I can help her."

"You're only a little boy," Mrs. Mannerd said. "I know you children have your fun pretending, but you are a child and so is she, and you'll understand one day that this is for the better."

Lionel was so frustrated that he screamed.

It was a sound that Mrs. Mannerd hated especially, and Lionel knew it. But this time, Mrs. Mannerd did not cover her ears or tell him to stop. She kept hold of his arm and she marched right into the house, past the poor tutor who had been nervously searching for Lionel all morning.

Lionel was still screaming when Mrs. Mannerd dragged him up the stairs and into her bedroom, which was strictly off-limits. This got Lionel to stop screaming. He had never seen what was on the other side of this door. None of the children had.

It smelled faintly of laundered clothes and talcum powder. Lionel didn't get a chance to look around the room before Mrs. Mannerd had opened the closet door and pushed him inside.

Stunned, he tried the knob, but it was jammed. He pounded on the door, kicked it, but it was solid wood and it hardly even rattled.

"I'm sorry," Mrs. Mannerd said. "I can't have you running after her. You'll only get yourself lost, or worse."

Lionel rattled the doorknob and screamed. He made his hands like claws and tried to dig his way through the wood, even after the silence on the other side told him that Mrs. Mannerd had gone.

Downstairs, Mrs. Mannerd took the flour from the pantry and rummaged through the box of recipes she kept in a shoe box by the stove. Her hands were shaking, and the only thing that had ever settled her nerves was to cook. Anything would do.

But she could hear Lionel stomping around upstairs, and it was impossible to concentrate on the recipes.

Despite the racket Lionel made, she was not thinking

about Lionel as much as she was thinking about Marybeth.

She turned on the oven.

By midafternoon, the older children had returned from school, and the house was filled with their noise. From the kitchen, Mrs. Mannerd could hear their silly chatter and their meaningless arguments. They did not even notice that Lionel and Marybeth were gone.

Upstairs in the closet, Lionel had curled up on the floor and was staring at the crack of light that came through from under the door.

He thought about the skeleton in the yellow dress, and what Marybeth said about the lost souls wandering on Halloween. He thought back to the way the blue creature had been able to put on Marybeth's boots and button her coat, and how it knew the way to the farmhouse.

The blue creature, when it was alive, had been a human girl. Just like Marybeth.

Lionel had hours to imagine what sorts of horrible things had happened to the blue creature that led to her body being buried in that shed. He thought of how frightened the blue creature was of strangers, the way it ran away and cried out when someone got too close to

Marybeth. The way it attacked the older one that took Marybeth's food.

The blue creature had been murdered. There was no question about that. Maybe, Lionel thought, he could free Marybeth and together they could bring the blue creature back to her body.

He wasn't sure how to get out of this closet, much less how to save Marybeth. But one thing he knew for certain was that he couldn't tell Mrs. Mannerd the truth. Even after seeing what the blue creature had done to Marybeth, she believed that Marybeth was sick. She would never believe the truth. And even if he showed Mrs. Mannerd the skeleton in the barn, she would call the police. The police would take the bones and the yellow dress away, and then the blue creature would never find its way back and Marybeth would be haunted forever.

Lionel stayed very silent. Maybe Mrs. Mannerd would open the door if she thought he was dead. And maybe, if he could mimic the blue creature, she would take him to the same place she'd taken Marybeth.

Late that evening, the older children sat down for supper, and Mrs. Mannerd prepared a plate to take to Lionel. She included a slice of raspberry pie, which she knew he loved and would probably eat even if he was mad at her. But just as she was about to walk upstairs, the telephone rang.

This caused the older children to stop their chatter. The phone never rang unless something big was about to happen, like a storm, or the arrival of a new orphan with nowhere left to go.

The ringing made Mrs. Mannerd very nervous, but she didn't let it show. She set Lionel's plate on the staircase, and she picked up the receiver and said, "Hello?"

CHAPTER 17

The closet door was yanked open, waking Lionel from his fitful dreams of empty dresses buried in shallow graves. Mrs. Mannerd was standing over him, holding his coat and boots. "Get dressed," she said, and the urgency in her voice made Lionel forget that he was angry with her. "We're going to get Marybeth."

Lionel was dressed and in the car before Mrs. Mannerd had even finished buttoning her coat.

The sky was dark now, and thunder rumbled in the distance. Mrs. Mannerd ran from the house, not bothering with the scarf she wore on her head when it rained. She must have been very worried.

She started the car and backed down the driveway

faster than Lionel thought the car had been able to go. Just as they turned onto the road, it started to rain.

Finally, Lionel said, "Marybeth is in trouble, isn't she?"

"She's gone missing," Mrs. Mannerd said. "I don't understand how. She was tied to the bed, and they said that she chewed through the restraints and somehow broke through the window."

The word "restraints" hit Lionel like a punch. How could Mrs. Mannerd let them put Marybeth in restraints?

He swallowed down his argument. If he didn't behave, she might not allow him to come along. Politeness had become such a habit in recent weeks that he didn't have to work very hard to speak rationally. He said, "Why are you letting me come with you?"

"Because she listens to you." Mrs. Mannerd shook her head. "I don't understand it, but you're the only one in the world who can talk to her these days."

The rain sounded like hands on the roof of the car banging to be let in. A flash of lightning illuminated the road before them.

Mrs. Mannerd muttered prayers. Lionel thought of Marybeth and the frightened blue creature out in the cold rain.

The drive was very long, even though Mrs. Mannerd drove faster than the car was meant to go. Near the end of the drive, Lionel was beginning to contemplate prayers himself.

The car turned onto the bumpy dark road that was lined with trees. Lionel's stomach lurched, not because of the turbulence, but because this scary road was one that Marybeth had taken.

There was nothing but blackness.

Lionel first saw the building when it was illuminated by a flash of lightning. He shrank back in his seat. No wonder the blue creature had run away.

Mrs. Mannerd stopped the car, but she didn't open her door right away. She gripped the steering wheel and took a deep breath. "Lionel," she said, "I want you to do what you have to do." She looked at him. "If you can find her, do what you have to do. You won't be in trouble."

Lionel nodded. They opened their doors and stepped out into the rain.

Lionel did not like the building at all. It smelled like open wounds, and the hallways were windowless cages.

The nurses were frantic and as white as their uniforms. They led Mrs. Mannerd and Lionel to the room where Marybeth had been.

Even for the blue creature, the sight was odd. There were leather straps at each corner of the bed, stretched and worn until they were big enough to escape from. The window was small and very high on the wall. The glass was smashed and framed by bloody shards. The wind howled through the opening.

"What in the world," Mrs. Mannerd gasped.

"I have seen a great many things," one of the nurses said, "but this—this isn't human."

"Yes it is," Lionel said.

When he spoke, it was the first time the nurses could bother to notice him. But they didn't get more than a glimpse, because in the next instant he had taken off running for the door.

It was a black moonless night, and once he had stepped outside, Lionel had little sense of where he was. The light from the building's window was faint.

He ran to the building's side first, to see where Marybeth would have escaped from her window.

There was a tree whose branches scraped against the brick. She must have climbed down from there, Lionel thought.

He was overwhelmed by the infiniteness of the woods and overpowered by the rain and cold, but he didn't care. He would search for her as long as it took. All night, if he had to.

And then he saw it. A flash of blue.

It darted through the trees.

"Wait!" Lionel called. His voice was taken by the wind. He ran through the trees, tripping on brambles and roots. "Wait! Marybeth, are you in there? Can you hear me?"

The blue light hesitated and froze in place, giving Lionel enough time for a closer look.

He was frightened by what he saw. There in the darkness, with one hand pressed against the trunk of a large tree, was Marybeth, glowing like a ghost. She was barefoot and wearing a torn white gown that was no defense against this weather. Blood stained her sleeve and her knees.

She was looking at him, with eyes as blue as the rest of her. And Lionel understood that this was not Marybeth. This was the elusive creature he had tracked for days to no avail, thinking it was a fox.

The creature stared at him a moment longer, and Lionel thought he saw recognition in its eyes. But then it was gone again, running into the darkness.

Lionel ran after it. He couldn't predict what the creature was capable of, nor did he understand how it was able to move so quickly. But he knew Marybeth. He knew that she was only human, and that the blue creature would run until Marybeth's body was spent and she died out here in this cold.

"Marybeth," he called.

Lightning flashed.

"Marybeth!"

At last he stopped to catch his breath. He'd lost all sense of where he was now. The building and its lights were no longer visible, nor was that eerie blue light.

The sound of the rain concealed the sound of Marybeth's footsteps, and he did not know where the blue creature had taken her.

He found a tree with enough footholds for him to climb, and he made his way to the top, clinging to the slick bark. Lightning flashed again, and the world went dark again when it was gone.

"Marybeth!" he called again, when he had climbed as high as the tree would allow. He searched for any trace of blue light, but there was nothing.

As he climbed back down, he began to realize that the water on his cheeks was not entirely from the rain.

Don't cry, he told himself.

Lions didn't cry.

Birds didn't cry.

Coyotes and tigers and mice didn't cry.

But try as he might, he could not run like a lion and cover the breadth of the woods. He could not fly above the trees and look down and find Marybeth. He had lost her, the way that only a silly, powerless human could lose something so important.

He began to shiver from the cold. He wouldn't go back without her. He would search until he could no longer stand. If she was lost, then he would be lost, too.

Just as he moved to take another futile step, there was a sound behind him.

He spun, and there was Marybeth, on her hands and knees in the mud, poised as though to attack. He could see her fighting behind those eerily glowing eyes. Her fingers were clawing into the ground. Her face twitched as she tried to speak.

She was the one who found her way to him, he realized. The blue creature was whimpering and thrashing its head, trying to resist.

He stayed where he was, with two yards of distance between them.

"It's okay," Lionel said, and held up his hands. "It's me. You remember me. I won't hurt you."

He could see the blue creature's conflict. It was frightened, but cold. It didn't want to stay out here, but it wouldn't go back into that awful building.

"You don't have to go back inside," Lionel said. He was shivering, but he kept his voice steady. "I won't let them leave you here. We can go back home. But you have to let Marybeth out."

The blue creature nursed its wounded hand.

Lionel took a cautious step closer, then another. The blue creature watched him.

Finally, he was close enough to see Marybeth's face clearly.

"I understand," Lionel told the blue creature. "I know why you kept running back to the barn. I know that someone killed you."

The blue creature snarled, not at Lionel, but at some memory his words evoked.

"We're the same, you and me," Lionel said. "You see how awful humans can be, and you would rather be anything else. You don't want to be a girl anymore. That's okay. You don't have to be."

The blue creature breathed fast, shallow breaths.

"I can help you," Lionel said. "But not alone. I need Marybeth back. Please. She isn't yours."

The blue creature looked at him, and then, in a blink, the blue glow faded away, and all that Lionel could see was Marybeth's pale skin. She raised her head, startled, as though breaking the surface after nearly drowning.

"L-Lionel?"

Lionel unbuttoned his coat and wrapped it around her, pulling up the collar in an attempt to shield her head from the rain. But it was no matter; she was already soaked through.

"It won't stay a-asleep for l-long." Her teeth were chattering, and she couldn't form more words.

"It's okay," Lionel said. "I'll help you. It's okay."

She stumbled when Lionel helped her to her feet, but she was able to move on wobbly legs until they made it back to the light coming from the open door to the building.

Mrs. Mannerd ran down the steps and ushered them inside. Once the door had been closed behind them, she knelt to look at Marybeth. Marybeth's braids were coming undone and her hair had bits of twigs in it. But there was none of that blue tinge Mrs. Mannerd had seen earlier. It must have been a trick of the light, Mrs. Mannerd told herself.

Lionel and Marybeth sat on the floor in the lobby, huddled in a blanket and holding warm cups of tea. Marybeth had changed out of that awful gown and was wearing a brown gingham dress that Mrs. Mannerd had packed for her in the hatbox. Her bloody arm had been washed out and then wrapped in a cloth bandage by rough nurses who were afraid to touch her. She had finally stopped shivering, but still she hadn't said a word.

Lionel stayed close by her side. Though the blue creature had hidden itself for now, he knew that it would be back. It always came back. Mrs. Mannerd was down the hall giving the nurses a piece of her mind for letting this happen, and Lionel knew he didn't have much time to talk to Marybeth alone.

"I've found where the blue creature is buried," he said quietly.

Marybeth looked at him. Her nose was running. She took a sip from her tea.

"You were right," he said. "The blue creature is a girl. Or at least, it was, when she was alive. Someone murdered her and buried her in the shed behind the farmhouse. I dug up the bones."

Marybeth drew her knees to her chest. "There's a boy with blue buttons for a face," she said. "I dream about him sometimes. I think that's the murderer." She looked at him. Her eyes were big and dark. "I don't want to find him."

"We just have to get you back to the farmhouse," Lionel said. "If we show the blue creature where her body is, maybe she'll go back to it."

"And then we tell the police," Marybeth said. "We have to. She should have a proper burial. Maybe that's all she wants."

Lionel was going to say more, but Marybeth put her head on his shoulder, and he knew that she was frightened. So all he said was, "Okay."

"She can't stay here," a woman down the hall was telling Mrs. Mannerd. "She's evil. She's inhuman."

"She's only a child," Mrs. Mannerd cried. "I made the awful mistake of trusting her to you in the first place. I wouldn't make it again for all the riches in the queen's palace."

Mrs. Mannerd stormed down the hall and took the cups of tea from Lionel's and Marybeth's hands and set them on the floor. "Come on, children. Come on, up, up, we're leaving."

Lionel and Marybeth didn't need to be told again. Still wrapped in the shared blanket, they jumped to their feet and followed Mrs. Mannerd out to the car.

Mrs. Mannerd sped down the dark road, hitting every bump and muttering curses.

Lionel and Marybeth were huddled under the blanket in the backseat, clinging to each other. "Stay down," Marybeth whispered to the blue creature, so quietly that no one else could hear. "Stay down, stay down, stay down." She sneezed, and Mrs. Mannerd glanced in the rearview mirror.

"Are you feeling sick?" Mrs. Mannerd asked. "Heaven knows how long you were out there—honestly, Marybeth, you used to have better sense."

"I'm all right, Mrs. Mannerd, thank you," Marybeth said, and sneezed again.

Lionel could feel the heat from the fever on her skin. She was shivering again. He was frightened, and for several minutes he contemplated what to do.

Marybeth must have been thinking about the same thing, because she whispered, "We should tell her."

Lionel hesitated. He pulled the blanket up so that their faces were shielded from Mrs. Mannerd. "Once we get home, we can run away to the farmhouse. I'll show you where the skeleton is."

"Lionel, no," Marybeth said, with heartbreaking practicality. "I won't make it."

"I'll carry you," he said. But Marybeth didn't have to plead her case. He already knew she was right.

Marybeth lowered the blanket. "Mrs. Mannerd?" she said. "We have something to tell you."

CHAPTER 18

Mrs. Mannerd did not believe them about the blue creature. Or, at least, she was trying not to. "It was a figment of your imagination," she said, looking at Marybeth in the mirror. "It was dark and you were in a panic after you fell into the river."

"I saw it, too," Lionel said.

"You also think that you can turn into a bear," Mrs. Mannerd reasoned.

Lionel climbed out of the blanket and leaned over Mrs. Mannerd's seat so that he could get a better look at her. She glanced between him and the road. "You've seen it," Lionel said. "I know you have."

"Lionel, sit back down. No more of this. I'm taking you both home, and, Marybeth, I'm calling the doctor first thing in the morning and praying you don't get pneumonia."

"What if we can prove it?" Lionel said. "What if we can prove that all of this is real, and that there is a blue creature?"

"If you can prove it, I'll dance on the kitchen table," Mrs. Mannerd said.

"Okay," Lionel said. "Don't take us straight home. Take us to the farmhouse. I'll prove everything."

He sat back in his seat, quite proud of himself. But his triumph was short lived when he saw Marybeth. She had wrapped herself more tightly in the blanket, and her eyes were as shiny as the wet glass of the car windows.

Lionel put his hands on her cheeks. Burning hot. She stared tiredly back at him.

"It's going to be okay," he said. "Trust me."

She curled up against him and closed her eyes.

It was a long drive home. Mrs. Mannerd kept stealing worried glances at Marybeth in the rearview mirror.

Lionel was doing his best not to be angry with the blue creature for what it had done to Marybeth. It was frightened, and tying a frightened thing down in a sterile room was of course going to cause it to panic.

But while Marybeth had this ghost inside her skin, she was only human, and the cold had been too much for her. Lionel had never seen her so tired and frail.

By the time they were close to home, and the buildings through the window began to look familiar, Marybeth was struggling to stay awake. She sat up straight, blinking hard.

Neither of the children were sure whether Mrs. Mannerd would give them their chance to prove the blue creature's existence. But when the red house approached, Mrs. Mannerd muttered, "Oh, what am I doing?" and drove straight past it.

When they reached the farmhouse, Mrs. Mannerd switched off the engine and turned around in her seat and said, "I hope you know this is trespassing. What is it that you have to show me?"

Lionel opened the door, and as Marybeth moved to follow him, Mrs. Mannerd said, "No, I won't have you back out in this rain catching your death."

"I have to," Marybeth said, with much authority. "Trust us."

Mrs. Mannerd wasn't given much choice. Marybeth wrapped the blanket around herself like a cloak and followed Lionel out into the night.

The rain had subsided, but the wind had picked up. Lionel moved slowly, holding up the tufts of blanket so Marybeth wouldn't trip. With Mrs. Mannerd on their heels, they made their way to the barn.

Mrs. Mannerd, at least for the moment, had stopped voicing her skepticisms as she followed them.

Lionel threw open the door to the barn, and he felt an awful sense of dread deep within his stomach. Marybeth bristled, and Lionel wondered if she felt it, too, but she only sneezed.

Mrs. Mannerd struck a match and lit the emergency lantern she kept in the car. And in the sudden light, both she and Lionel were stricken by Marybeth's appearance.

Her eyes were sunken, with pale blue bags beneath them. The part of her hair was blue.

Lionel took her hand and led her deeper into the barn. When he reached the softened earth, he picked up the shovel and began the awful task of digging.

"Lionel, this is not our property," Mrs. Mannerd said.

"Let him," Marybeth said. "Please." She was too tired to stand, and she leaned against the wall.

Lionel felt the bone against the shovel, and he closed his eyes as he unearthed the next heap of dirt. When he finally allowed himself to open them, he could see the yellow dress, exactly where he'd left it.

Marybeth moved away from the wall. The blanket fell to a puddle at her feet as she marched toward the shallow grave.

With a heavy heart, Lionel unearthed the hollow skull.

"Heavens," Mrs. Mannerd whispered.

The blue glow was back in Marybeth's eyes. She dropped to her knees and reached into the grave.

"Marybeth, don't," Mrs. Mannerd said. But Marybeth was far away by then. There was only the blue creature, and when it saw what was left of its body, it let out a cry that no living thing could make.

Marybeth saw what the blue creature saw. She was inside its body, seeing through its eyes.

Lionel and Mrs. Mannerd were gone. The shallow grave and the bones were gone. The blue creature was wearing the yellow dress.

The dress was much brighter here, and it swished when the blue creature moved.

Marybeth watched as though she were in someone else's dream. The blue creature had the hands of a girl, and she pushed open the door to the barn, and a voice called out, "Liza!"

The blue creature turned its head toward the woods, where a boy in suspenders was wielding an ax.

The blue creature loved the boy. Marybeth could feel it in its heart. But not in the way that she loved Lionel. There was something different, something Marybeth had to search for before she understood. The blue creature loved the boy the way that Marybeth had, so long ago, loved her father. Like family.

She found that part of the blue creature's heart and she lingered there, enjoying the sensation of it. Family. It was a rare, musical word in her world.

The blue creature ran to him, the yellow dress fluttering against her legs. Always running. The blue creature hated to be still, even in death.

The blue creature reached the boy, her brother, and everything went dark.

Marybeth heard the blue creature scream. She felt it in its lungs. She tasted blood, felt the blue creature's legs breaking.

When the light came back, Marybeth saw blurred faces. The blue creature's mouth filled with water, and when it looked up it saw only one face. The boy, her brother, and then her eyes were covered by water, and his face blurred into blue marbles, with dark sockets for eyes.

CHAPTER 19

Marybeth tried to scream, but all that came out was a feeble cry.

The blue marble face turned into Lionel, whose eyes were big and concerned. She was lying in the dirt, and she struggled to move but her head felt too heavy to lift.

"Marybeth!" Mrs. Mannerd cried. She wrapped her in the blanket and lifted her up into her arms. "That's it, I'm getting you home and phoning the doctor."

Lionel had to pace to keep up with Mrs. Mannerd, she was moving so fast. "You can't," he said. "They'll take it away."

Mrs. Mannerd didn't stop, and she didn't answer. All she said was, "Get in the car," and her tone was so frightening that Lionel listened.

Marybeth closed her eyes and tried to finish the dream the blue creature had shown her in the barn.

"Liza?" she whispered. Her head felt as though it was full of wind. There was no answer.

As soon as they returned to the house, Mrs. Mannerd made a makeshift bed for Marybeth on the couch. Lionel sat on the floor beside her, straining to listen to the words Mrs. Mannerd was saying into the phone out in the hall. But for once, he couldn't hear any of it. He was too distracted by Marybeth's sniffling and chattering teeth. She was murmuring things that faded into incoherence.

Marybeth's hair was turning blue. It was a slight change, and it could be mistaken for a trick of the light, but Lionel knew it was only going to get worse. "It's not gone, is it?" he said, when she opened her eyes.

"No," Marybeth said. She was so very tired. "But I know her name now. It was Liza."

"Liza," Lionel echoed. It was such a normal, sensible name for such a destructive thing.

"I think she was murdered," Marybeth said. "But I don't know what happened. Everything went black."

"Try and think," Lionel said. "What did you see?"

"The farmhouse," Marybeth said. "And her brother. Maybe he was just a little older than we are. But I never saw anyone like that at the farmhouse, did you?"

An instinctive growl left Lionel's throat. "Reginald," he said. "The old woman's son."

Marybeth's eyes widened. "You're right."

"You said the blue creature hated him. That's it. He killed her."

"He killed his sister?" Marybeth shook her head against her pillow. "No, that can't be it. She loved him. I felt it."

"Just because you love someone doesn't mean they can't hurt you," Lionel said.

Marybeth's tired face gave way to concern. "I heard what you said in the woods," she told him. "You said that you and the blue creature are the same. You said that you both know how awful humans can be. What did you mean?"

Lionel turned away from her.

"Lionel," Marybeth said.

He growled, not at her but at the memory she was reviving.

Marybeth leaned over the edge of the couch and petted his hair. "You can tell me," she said.

A clap of thunder shook the house. The grandfather clock rattled against the wall.

Mrs. Mannerd came into the room with a thermometer. "I can't get ahold of anybody at this hour, but I'm going to keep trying. Are you feeling any better?" She stuck the thermometer into Marybeth's mouth before she could answer.

Marybeth's head lolled against the pillow like it was suddenly too heavy for her neck. Lionel was not sure whether the cold or the blue creature was to blame, or both, but he feared either way that she was dying.

Dying. The word was an echo in the darkest cave of his mind.

Mrs. Mannerd withdrew the thermometer and frowned at it. She left the room and came back with a spoon of foul-smelling medicine that Marybeth dutifully took.

After Mrs. Mannerd had gone, Lionel crawled onto the couch and sat at her feet.

Marybeth could not stay awake no matter how she tried, and after she had been asleep for several minutes, Lionel whispered, "Liza?"

There was no answer.

"I think you can hear me," Lionel said. "I think you're faking it."

Marybeth's eyelashes fluttered.

"Those are your bones in the barn. Maybe you don't like it, but that's you. Marybeth needs her own body back. What will happen if you kill her? You aren't sharing a body with me. I'll throw you back in the river if you try."

Marybeth's raspy breathing gave way to an angry hiss.

"I'll do it," Lionel said. "You kill Marybeth, I throw you back in that river for good. But if you come out now, I'll help you."

It was quiet for a long time, save for the thunder and the rain.

Marybeth gasped in her sleep.

The dream returned.

This time, Marybeth was no longer sharing a body with the blue creature. She had no body at all. She was the wind that moved through the trees. She was invisible and she saw everything.

Liza was not a frightening blue creature. She was a girl just like Marybeth, with braided pigtails and a yellow dress.

"Here," Reginald said. "You hold the ax, and I'll show you how to do it."

Though Marybeth did not share a body with Liza in this dream, she heard heavy footsteps crushing twigs in the woods, and she felt Liza's fear.

The boys that skulked into the clearing were as tall as Reginald, and they didn't have names or faces—only dark and sinister eyes.

Liza clutched the ax in her unsteady fingers. "Get out of here," she said, in a voice that was very brave despite the fear churning her stomach. "I said I'd tell my mother if you came back here. I know what you did to our hens."

"Liza, shut up," Reginald said. He was the one who sounded frightened.

The boys moved closer. There were three of them, but it felt as though there were a hundred.

"Go back to the house," Reginald told Liza.

"No," she said. "I'm not leaving you alone."

"Don't be stupid. Go inside."

One of the boys grabbed Liza by the arms, and the ax left her grip and fell to her feet with a hard sound of metal hitting dirt. The boy's face was nothing but dark eyes and snarling teeth, like something rabid. "She isn't going inside," the boy said. "She isn't going anywhere just yet."

A blue light began to glow under Marybeth's skin, dull at first, and then so bright that Lionel could see her bones. He could see her lungs breathing in and out. He could see the throbbing shadow of her heart. And beside that heart, he could see the blue creature's heart, the source of all that light, glowing as it beat to its own fast rhythm.

The glow became so bright that it hurt to look at, and he had to close his eyes.

He opened them again when he heard a skittering noise against the floorboards.

The blue glow had left Marybeth's skin. Now, the glow came from the floor, where the blue creature was huddled on its haunches. It looked, at first, like the fox Lionel had chased through the woods all those weeks ago, but now he was finally able to get a good look at it. What he had thought to be a foxtail was instead very long hair, which wrapped around the blue creature's huddled legs. Its eyes were big and glowing, but they were human.

"There now," Lionel said, and slowly slid from the couch to the floor. "Was that so hard?"

Marybeth stirred, and a moment later, she opened her eyes. It was the emptiness that woke her. A stillness where another heart had been beating.

The blue creature looked between Marybeth and Lionel. It was frightened, but it didn't run.

Cooing and mumbling soothing words, Lionel reached out. His hand went right through the blue creature, but he could feel coldness, as though he were sticking his hand out the window on a windy winter night.

Marybeth coughed and sniffled, and crawled off the couch to kneel beside Lionel. And there the three of them remained for a while, staring at each other, trying to make sense of what they saw.

Aside from the darting flashes of light through the woods and the reflection in the river, this was the first time Marybeth was able to get a good look at the thing that had been sharing a body with her. Despite the surreal glow, it was the same girl she had just dreamed. She was even wearing a dress.

"Can you talk, Liza?" Marybeth asked.

The blue creature shivered and hugged its knees.

"I saw what happened to you," Marybeth said. "Those boys in the woods hurt you, and then they left you in the river to drown, is that it?"

Though she was ordinary again, and her body was her own, Marybeth did not feel the same way she had before she met the blue creature. The blue creature did not speak, but Marybeth could hear her just the same. Her mind filled with memories that belonged to Liza.

She saw the farmhouse when its paint was fresh and new. She saw the old woman much younger, setting a plate of eggs before a man who was reading the newspaper.

She saw Reginald, as a young boy, coming down the stairs in his pajamas.

"They were your family, weren't they?" Marybeth asked. "The farmhouse was where you lived."

Hesitantly, the blue creature nodded. The gesture made her look human.

"He's the one who murdered you," Lionel said.

The blue creature looked at him sharply, her eyes throbbing with light. She shook her head frantically.

Lightning filled the room, and for an instant, the blue creature turned translucent in the flash.

The blue creature looked at Marybeth. Marybeth at once felt very tired, and her head lolled back and forth, and she closed her eyes.

She saw what the blue creature saw. The boy grabbed her arms, and she screamed. It was a human scream. A girl's scream.

Reginald reached for the ax, but it was too late. One of the other boys had already taken hold of it.

Marybeth awoke with a start. Lionel was watching her face very closely. "What did you see?" he asked.

Marybeth looked at the blue creature. "Your brother— Reginald. He tried to stop them? But he couldn't."

The blue creature nodded sadly.

"But why would they do something so awful?" Marybeth said.

The blue creature didn't answer. Marybeth searched her memories, but there wasn't an explanation.

Marybeth crawled closer to the blue creature. "Your mother doesn't know what happened to you. She doesn't know that you've been in the barn all this time. She's been looking for you."

The blue creature nodded.

"It's taken you this long to find someone you could trust," Lionel said. "See? I told you that we would help if you'd just be reasonable."

Lightning filled the room again, and once it passed, the blue creature had disappeared.

Marybeth shivered and coughed. Lionel helped her back onto the couch and tucked the blanket under her chin.

"She's gone," Marybeth said. "I still don't understand. Why was she buried in the barn? What does she want me to do?"

Lionel petted her hair. He could feel her fever through her scalp. "You should go to sleep," he said. "I'll wake you if the blue creature comes back."

"Liza," Marybeth murmured, as her eyelids grew too heavy to hold up. "Her name was Liza."

CHAPTER 20

By the time the sun came up, Marybeth's fever had gotten worse. She slept fitfully, dreaming the blue creature's memories and muttering words that made no sense in the waking world.

Lionel lay curled at her feet, waiting to see if the blue creature would return. She had left sometime before the clock struck midnight and hadn't returned.

Mrs. Mannerd paced in and out of the room with her thermometer and damp cloths, wringing her hands anxiously and then trying to place a call on the telephone over and over.

When there was a knock at the front door, Marybeth flinched and opened her eyes. She still felt the emptiness from where the blue creature had been. The only one there to greet her was Lionel. He would never leave her, she knew.

"Liza still hasn't come back?" she asked.

He shook his head.

There was a man's voice in the other room, and Marybeth squinted at the doorway. Now that the blue creature was gone, her vision was blurry without her spectacles. Her ordinary life didn't feel quite the same as it had just a few weeks earlier.

"I'll need to speak to the children who found it," the voice said.

"Is that truly necessary?" Mrs. Mannerd said. "They're resting now."

"It'll only be for a moment."

The man had boots that made a loud sound against the floorboards as he walked.

Lionel and Marybeth sat up straight as the man entered the room. He was dressed in a policeman's uniform.

"Which one of you found the skeleton?"

"We both did," Marybeth said. She was sniffling and dabbing her nose with a handkerchief, but it was best for her to do the talking. She was better at sounding normal than Lionel was. "We know we aren't supposed to play out there, but we couldn't help it. None of the

older kids could find us there, and we wanted them to leave us alone."

There was something about Marybeth's helpless state that caused the policeman to soften. "Have you told anyone else about what you found?"

"Only Mrs. Mannerd," she said. "We're sorry. We won't go out there again."

The policeman cleared his throat. "That's quite all right. It'll all be taken care of now."

After the policeman was gone, Marybeth sank against the couch and closed her eyes.

Lionel hovered anxiously over her. "Is it really gone?" he asked.

"I think so. I can't feel anything."

When she began to fall asleep, he sat on the floor beside her.

He took her hand, and she smiled with her eyes closed.

The doctor came by in the late morning and shooed Lionel from the room, telling him that Marybeth was too contagious for him to be exposed. But Lionel wouldn't get sick. He knew he wouldn't. Years of hiding outdoors and sleeping under a drafty roof had gotten him used to the cold.

Once the doctor had gone, Lionel returned to the living room to resume his vigil.

Even pale and tired, Marybeth was fierce. Unafraid. When she opened her eyes, they were filled with determination. After weeks of being subject to the blue creature's whims, she finally had her own skin to herself and she wanted to be awake for it.

"You've done such a good job being human all these weeks," she said hoarsely. "I've enjoyed it."

"Don't get used to it," he said.

"Lionel." She rolled onto her side to look at him. "Is it so awful being human?"

He sat on the floor, tugging at a loose thread in her blanket. "There are better things to be."

She propped herself up on her elbow and looked at him. "Why?" she said. "Why would you rather be a gosling, or a bear, or a squirrel than a boy?"

He bristled. No one had ever asked him such a thing. The closest anyone came was when Mrs. Mannerd put her hands on her hips and said, "Why can't you sit at the table with the rest of us?" or "Why must you test me today of all days?"

That last one was her favorite, and she said it a lot.

But Marybeth was looking at him with sincere curiosity, and it frightened him.

"It was a long time ago," he said. "It isn't important."

"Did someone hurt you?" she went on with graceful persistence. "The way someone hurt Liza."

Lionel pulled his knees against his chest and tried to look away, but he couldn't. He couldn't hide from Marybeth the way that he hid from everyone else.

"I'm not a real orphan," he confessed. "My mother is dead, but my father isn't. He's in jail. But he isn't coming out, so it's like he's dead."

Marybeth slid off the couch and sat on the floor beside him. She brought the blanket with her, and fitted it around the both of them.

She was so close that he could feel the warmth of her fever. She said, "Why is he in jail?"

The question was more than a question. It was a fast journey down a winding road, to a place Lionel didn't want to visit again. Not ever again.

"He was never all the way awake," Lionel said. "He drank all day. I used to think that the stuff in those bottles was his blood, and he needed it to live. I used to see the liquid shining in the bottles and hope it would be enough for him to see tomorrow."

Marybeth listened.

"My mother—all I remember is that she wore a green dress and her hair was short, and she was always mad at him. That's it. That's all I remember. She always had a green dress on. That's the way she died."

Marybeth's voice was soft. "What happened to her?"

Lionel had never felt so painfully human. He wanted

to grow wings. He wanted the wings to tear through his skin and fluff out, bloody and full and strong, and carry him away.

"It turns out that it wasn't blood in the bottles," he said. "It was poison. The worst kind of poison there is. It made him see things. Think things. It made him mean."

He shivered, and Marybeth took his hands. "Lionel," she whispered.

She understood. That was her gift, Lionel thought; she didn't need to see horrible things to understand that they existed. Compassion was just a part of her way. She wasn't going to ask him to tell the rest of the story, but now he had to. If he didn't, it would stay trapped in his throat, forever waiting to be spoken.

"He killed her," Lionel said. "They fought until he had her down on the floor and he put his hands around her neck. I couldn't make him stop. I didn't have any claws. I didn't have any fangs. All I could do was hide."

"Shh," Marybeth said, because she heard the tremor in his voice before he did. She put her arms around him, and he could feel her heart beating against his own chest.

It was no wonder the blue creature had hidden within her. She was a fortress. She was the only safe place in a world of frightening strangers.

"Shh," she said again, and rocked him. "It's okay, I'm here."

He was grateful that he was human, if only for a moment, if only for now.

Two weeks went by, and Marybeth began to feel better. In truth she didn't mind being in quarantine. Mrs. Mannerd brought her tea and toast with jam, and the older ones were afraid to get close to her.

The hollow feeling under her skin began to lessen, as though her organs were settling back into place, making her something normal again.

During her evening bath, she soaked in the warm water and tried to conjure up a memory of the blue creature being pushed into the river. But it was gone.

"Liza? If you're frightened, you can still come to me for help," she said. And after thinking about it, she added, "Just stay on the outside this time."

There was no answer, and she worried for the blue creature, frightened and alone somewhere. She worried about what would happen to its bones.

Lionel kept close to her and asked if there were any signs of it. Every time, the answer was no.

As Marybeth grew healthier, Lionel asked about the blue creature less and less. Mrs. Mannerd had also stopped giving Marybeth her worried glances. Life began to return to normal, and with each passing day, it came to be as though the blue creature had never happened.

For everyone but Marybeth, that is. Though the hollow feeling inside her chest was mostly gone, a bit of it never healed up completely, and she got a sense that there was something that needed to be finished.

The day that Marybeth finally stopped sneezing, she began to sense that Liza was nearby. It was as though her ghost had been waiting for her to be strong enough to hear her.

It was as the older ones were rushing downstairs for breakfast. Marybeth lingered on the top step with her hand on the bannister. She didn't move. She waited for the older ones to pass her and for it to be quiet enough to listen.

"Liza?" Marybeth's voice was barely a whisper.

She didn't see Liza, nor did she feel her under her skin. But a thought had been planted in her mind. She had to speak to Reginald. There was something more to do.

"Marybeth?" Mrs. Mannerd was staring up at her. "You need to eat your breakfast and keep up your strength. We don't want a relapse."

Marybeth looked around her. Liza was nowhere, and still the thought of Liza's brother persisted.

"Yes, Mrs. Mannerd," she said.

CHAPTER 21

Liza's funeral was on a day made gray and white by winter.

There was no one to attend, except for Liza's mother and Reginald, and the man who read from the Bible, and the gravedigger who removed his hat and leaned on his shovel.

Marybeth and Lionel didn't approach. They stood by the entrance and watched. From here, death was not so immediate. None of the gravestones seemed to have names, and the ground was soft and white.

The hollow in Marybeth's chest was more noticeable today. She watched the funeral and felt horribly sad. Little girls shouldn't have funerals at all, but if they did, they should be filled with people who had loved her.

There should have been more than just bones to bury.

Lionel grabbed her hand, and his touch reminded her that there were still living things in the world. It wasn't all ghosts and muttered prayers.

The man closed the Bible and the old woman started crying. That was it. There were no more words to be said.

Marybeth hesitated, then she let go of Lionel's hand. "I'm going to talk to Reginald."

"Are you sure?" Lionel said. For him, the wild blue creature had been tamed. She was where she belonged, and she hadn't come back.

But Marybeth knew that the emptiness wouldn't go away until she knew everything that Liza had wanted to tell her.

"I'll be back," she said. "Wait here."

She stepped into the cemetery, but she didn't have to go much farther. Reginald had seen her, and he met her by the entrance.

He was a tall man, with a face as sullen and gray as the clouds that loomed overhead. But Liza had shown Marybeth how he once looked as a boy. As she still remembered him even now.

"Does your family know you're out here?" he said. "They must be missing you."

With that, Marybeth realized that she knew more about Reginald than he knew about her. She had seen the most horrible moment of his entire life, played out before her like a dream. But to him, she was just a peculiar child who kept sneaking into his barn.

"We were just walking to the library," she said. This was the truth, but not all of it. Nobody had told Marybeth that Liza would be buried today, but she had sensed it and knew that she needed to come. "And we— I, I wanted to say I'm sorry."

Reginald smiled, but it was a distracted, sad smile. He looked over his shoulder at his mother weeping by the open grave, and then he looked at Marybeth. "Did you see my sister?" he asked. "I've always thought she haunted the woods, but I never saw her. Sometimes I thought I was crazy."

"Yes," Marybeth said. "She told me that you tried to protect her. I think she was tired of being a ghost and she wanted to rest."

Reginald ran his hand through his hair. For a moment he looked just like a young boy.

"Why was she buried in the barn?" Marybeth asked. If Mrs. Mannerd were here, she'd scold her for asking such a forward question. But the blue creature had made her brave.

But Reginald wasn't bothered by the question. "You remind me of her," he said. "Fearless."

A few weeks ago, nobody would have described Mary-beth as bold. She had been cautious and polite. But she was learning now that she had more bravery than she knew.

"Liza was our mother's favorite," Reginald said. "Liza made her happier than anything in the world. Even when we were kids, I could see that. Our father saw it, too. So we protected her as best we could. But—you're young yet, but one day you'll learn that sometimes things happen."

Marybeth already knew this, but she let him go on.

"Liza had drowned by the time I was able to pull her out of the water. I tried, but there wasn't anything I could do."

Marybeth felt the hollowness throbbing in her chest, filling with sorrow.

"Burying her in the barn was our father's idea," Regi-nald said. "He said it would be easier on my mother if she didn't know what happened. If she thought Liza had run off or been kidnapped—anything would be better than the truth."

Something caught Marybeth's eye. Behind Reginald, by the open grave, there was a bit of blue light in the sun's ray. It touched the sobbing old woman's shoulder.

The old woman didn't see it, but as the blue light morphed into a translucent blue girl, she raised her head.

But even if the old woman didn't see it, Lionel had. He stepped to Marybeth's side, as though to protect her if the blue creature had any ideas about coming back.

"I always felt that she was still around somewhere," Reginald said. "But it's been nearly forty years. It's time for her to sleep now."

"I think she will," Marybeth said.

A cloud drifted apart from the others, creating a tear in the grayness and allowing the sun to poke through. In the light, the blue creature's glow was faint—almost invisible. And then it was gone.

ACKNOWLEDGMENTS

Writing acknowledgments is always more difficult than writing the story itself; as they say, the truth is stranger than fiction, and I will always find it very strange that there are so many wonderful people who continue to support me and my stories on the good days, the not-so-good days, and the stick-the-laptop-in-the-toaster days.

To my family, the living and the no longer living: thank you for a lifetime of support and love. Especially to Riley and Mary, who let me read pieces of this story to them at Thanksgiving and kept asking what happens next.

Thank you to the greatest support system I could ever have, for telling me that writing is a good idea, even on days when I did not feel it was so: Beth Revis, who comes first even though these names are listed in no particular order, and who makes me laugh the best. Harry Lam, who knows everything. Aprilynne Pike, who is practical. Randi Oomens, who encourages me. To Laura Bickle, Renée Ahdieh, Samantha Shannon, Leigh Bardugo, Aimée Carter, and Jodi Meadows, who are too talented. To Laini Taylor, who seems to think soy bacon is a good idea. To Sabaa Tahir, who is the brightest lighthouse beam.

Thanks, as always, to my agent, Barbara Poelle, whose level of enthusiasm and support is frightening every time. And to my wonderful editor, Cat Onder, for continuing to believe in these little worlds I write. Another huge thank you to Donna Mark and Colleen Andrews for creating a cover that just defies all I could dare to dream. Thank you to the entire team at Bloomsbury for being with me on this journey.

What if a machine could bring back the ones we love?

Read on for a sneak peek at **Lauren DeStefano**'s next haunting and heartfelt novel.

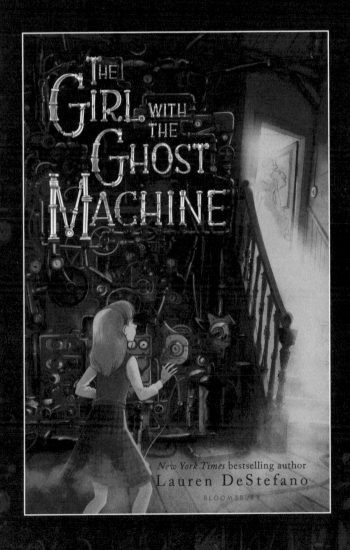

New York Times bestselling author
Lauren DeStefano

Bloomsbury

Emmaline Beaumont was ten and one quarter when her father started building the ghost machine. It was one month after her mother's funeral exactly.

To some, the pursuit of ghosts might have seemed greedy, given all that life had to offer. There was no shortage of living things in the world, to be sure. Even the rabbits that chewed through their vegetable garden, the chipmunks that left holes in the dirt, the Rousseau family across the alley whose records played at all

hours and whose children drew pictures in the fog of their breath on every window from Saint Laurent street to the school.

But when Emmaline's mother, Margeaux Beaumont, died, it seemed as though everything else had died with her. Emmaline and her father could no longer see the colors in the trees. They could no longer hear the melody in music. The vegetable garden became overrun by weeds, and the carrots and the tomatoes turned gray and shriveled.

Emmaline herself hardly spoke in the first month after her mother's death, sustaining herself on the chocolate cherries her mother kept hidden under the sink, salting them with her tears.

Every day since her mother's death, Emmaline wore a single black lace glove on her left hand, closest to her heart.

The curtains were always drawn, and the house was always dark.

This was before Emmaline's father got the idea for the ghost machine.

One day, two months after Emmaline's mother had died, and neither Emmaline nor her father had left the house but to retrieve the mail, Mademoiselle Chaveau, who taught at the school, hammered the iron knocker on the door until at last someone answered.

"Enough of this now, enough," Mademoiselle Chaveau had cried. "You can't have that child living in a morgue. She needs to be in school."

And so Emmaline returned to her lessons, and when she came home in the afternoons, sunlight filled her light honey-colored hair. The smell of autumn burrowed in the fibers of her sweater. She was brimming with jokes and whispers and giggles she had collected all day like stones in her pockets.

And it was then, just as life had begun to make sense to Emmaline again, that the ghost

machine came about. She returned from school one afternoon to find her father in the basement, crouched over scraps of metal and foraging through jars of bolts and rusted nails.

Soon thereafter, Julien became the subject of whispers and rumors on Saint Laurent street. He shuttered himself in the basement for hours each day, and all anyone heard was the clang and clatter of machinery and the occasional muttered curse.

Some believed the loss of his wife had driven him mad. Neighbors would knock on the door, bearing covered dishes and freshly baked treats, all hoping to catch a glimpse of whatever he did in that gloomy house. But if he answered the door at all, it was never for more than a fleeting moment, just long enough to mutter a word of thanks.

At ten and one quarter years old, Emmaline was old enough to know that a ghost machine wasn't a very realistic idea. The world was filled with bolts and gears and flickering light bulbs, and if these things could somehow summon ghosts, it surely would have happened by now.

But still, she had hoped, despite all reason, that it might work. The house was quiet and lonely without her mother to straighten its picture frames and draw its curtains and fill the rooms up with her humming. Now, dishes piled in the sink, and the kitchen table was littered with bills and cards expressing sympathy, and an uncapped jar of honey whose contents had dribbled out onto the week-old newspaper resting beneath it.

And though the idea of summoning ghosts sounded rather odd, Emmaline knew also that there was nothing odd about her father. Rather, he had loved her mother very much. Margeaux Beaumont had left them quite suddenly, after a short and unexpected illness, and there simply hadn't been time to prepare for such tremendous sorrow. When Margeaux died, her coffee cup was still in the sink, soaking in pink

suds that shined and shimmered. Her slippers were neatly placed near the bathtub, and an oval nest of her fine gold hair was still caught in the brush beside the bathroom sink.

And so, when her father began collecting pieces for the machine, Emmaline helped him. She brought him little rusted gears and nails—things she found on the side of the road mostly—and discarded paper clips that were bent out of shape. She collected and rinsed out empty marmalade jars and cans, all the while knowing that these mundane things could not possibly bring her mother back to her. Even so, that small bit of hope was what made her go on foraging for supplies.

One afternoon she pushed an old deflated tire up the steps. Her father was so pleased by this offering that he hugged her until her feet left the ground and he twirled her across the kitchen and kissed the top of her hair.

That was when she asked him, "Papa, what will this machine do?"

His answer was simple. "It will summon ghosts."

"But *how*, Papa?"

"Think of the puddles in the street after it rains," her father said. "Where do they go?"

"I suppose they disappear," Emmaline answered.

He tapped her nose. "They don't disappear. They evaporate. The clouds gather them up, and when it's time, they come back again as rain. Your mother is just like that."

"Mama is in a cloud?" Emmaline asked, skeptical.

"She's not in a cloud, exactly," her father said. "But she's somewhere out there, where things go when it seems like they've disappeared. She can't come back and live with us because her body is gone now, but bodies aren't the most important part of us. The special part, the true part, evaporates when we die. This machine will bring that part back. As to how it will work, that is a small matter to sort

out." Her father waved his hand as though swatting away a fly. "It will all make sense once it's done. You'll see."

At first, the machine was strictly off limits. Emmaline would hear her father tinkering and toiling—very rarely shouting, often grumbling—behind the closed door of the basement. Emmaline had never particularly liked the basement. It was dark and damp and full of spiders. But whenever she brought her father pieces for his machine, she found herself trying to peer into the dark stairwell over his shoulder, wanting to catch a glimpse of this thing that had come to consume him. But he always closed the door before she could see.

With time, her father became as inaccessible as the machine. He stopped answering the door when she knocked. He was still in the basement when Emmaline returned from school in the afternoons. At 3:05 precisely, she would leave a sandwich on a plate at the top of the stairs. She would knock on the basement door only once, for she knew her father would know what it meant.

Sometimes her father would retrieve the sandwich promptly. But sometimes—in fact, most times—the sandwich was still there in the evening when Emmaline emerged from her bath and had begun to prepare for bed.

"Good night, Papa," Emmaline would say on such occasions.

The only response would be the clatter and clamor of tools and gears.

Faced with the quiet of an empty house, Emmaline began to grieve for her father as well. He was still alive, but he was as gone as the dead for as little as she saw of him.

Late one night, kept awake by the thunking and banging in the basement, she climbed out of bed and made her way to the basement, and threw open the door.

Her father didn't notice at first, lost as he was in his work. He didn't hear her until she had reached the bottom step.

And just like that, Emmaline had her first look at the thing that had taken up all her father's time. The thing into which he had poured all his hopes. The thing he believed would bring Margeaux back.

Even though the thing did not work—had never worked—Emmaline was rendered speechless by the sight of it. It was a hulking thing, nearly as high as the ceiling. It was a great metal monster, with hundreds of bolts for eyes, and a rectangular mouth, into which Emmaline supposed something was meant to be deposited the way old clothes were deposited into a donation bin.

The basement itself was dark, but the ghost machine created its own light once Emmaline reached the bottom step. A flickering, eerie purple glow that came through all the cracks and corners of the fused metal.

It was unlike anything Emmaline had ever seen. She wouldn't know how to describe such a thing, much less how to describe the way it made her feel betrayed by her own sense of logic. She knew what machines were supposed to look like. She knew what death meant, and that ghosts weren't real. But this machine, frightening and amazing at the same time, made her feel as though anything was possible. It might even be possible for her mother's ghost to emerge from that peculiar glow.

She had expected her father to be angry with her for bursting into the basement, but when he saw the look of wonder on her face, he only smiled.

It had been two years since the start of the ghost machine's assembly now. Emmaline was twelve and one quarter, and half a foot taller, and the machine still did not work.

Emmaline didn't understand how it would ever work, or why it ate up so much electricity. She kept it a secret, fearing her father would be deemed mad and she would be taken from him.

It had been two years since Emmaline first laid eyes on the ghost machine, and it hadn't been much discussed with her father since.

But it was always there, even if Emmaline rarely was able to go down to the basement and have a good look at it. The ghost machine had become sort of like a stepmother to her, Emmaline thought, the way her father lavished it with affection. The ghost machine took and took her father's love, and offered nothing in return. Even the hope once implied by its presence was gone.

It took two years for Emmaline to work up the nerve to say what she had been thinking for a very long time. She planned it very carefully, turning the words over and over in her head, and then whispering them to her bedroom mirror that morning, until they were smoothed and polished as a stone.

She took a deep breath and then descended the stairs. Mornings were the only opportunity she would have to speak to her father. It was a very short window before he disappeared into the basement, where he would still be until long after she'd gone to bed.

He was at the kitchen table, his elbow resting on a scant three inches of clear space amid the clutter, sipping tea and staring at the newspaper in his lap. The paper was a week old, but the fact that he was reading about the outside world at all was a good sign, Emmaline thought.

"Papa," she said, her voice strong and clear. She straightened the hemline of her jumper. "I have something to tell you."

Her father barely afforded her a glance. "You should have breakfast," he said. "There are some bananas on the counter."

"They've gone bad," Emmaline said. "Papa, it's about the machine. I'd like you to unplug it."

At last, her father looked up from his paper. He set down his tea.

"Unplug it?"

Now that she had her father's attention, Emmaline felt all the words she had planned escaping her. They flew right out of her head and fluttered away.

She stood up straighter.

"It would be for the best," she said. "Mama is—gone—" That word caught in her throat. Even after two years, she would never be used to the idea that her mother wasn't coming home, and it felt wrong to say. She went on, "And she wouldn't want you to spend all your time in the basement trying to bring her back."

"She isn't gone," her father said, his voice soft and gentle, as if he were reading her a bedtime story. "She's somewhere, but she can't find her way back to us. That's all. The machine will help her find a way, like a lighthouse beam."

Emmaline could feel herself shaking, deep down in her bones. Her head felt foggy, the way it always did when she was about to cry.

Don't cry, she told herself. *Remember what you practiced.* But she could no longer remember the words she had practiced. It was far easier to come up with a good argument when she was alone in her bedroom. But here, faced

with her father's stubbornness, she remembered all at once why she hadn't brought this matter up at all in the past two years. It didn't matter what she said. He would never listen.

"Mama isn't 'somewhere,'" Emmaline said firmly. "She's in the cemetery, with about a hundred other people, and none of them are going to come back. None of them are ever going to come back, Papa. Everyone in the world knows that's what it means when people die. Everyone except for you."

"Everyone knew that light came from candles," her father said, still in that dulcet tone. "If everyone had accepted that, we would never have light bulbs. We would never have electricity at all. The solution is there, Emmaline. It just takes someone brave enough to find it."

He frowned and reached for her hands, and that's the moment Emmaline realized that she had started to cry. She knew that she had lost, that she would always lose when it came to that machine.

Lauren DeStefano is the *New York Times* and *USA Today* bestselling author of *A Curious Tale of the In-Between*; *The Peculiar Night of the Blue Heart*; *The Girl with the Ghost Machine*; the Internment Chronicles; and the Chemical Garden trilogy, which includes *Wither*, *Fever*, and *Sever*. She earned her BA in English with a concentration in creative writing from Albertus Magnus College in Connecticut.

www.laurendestefano.com

laurendestefano.tumblr.com

@LaurenDeStefano

PRAM'S BEST FRIEND HAS ALWAYS BEEN A GHOST . . .

Don't miss this unforgettable tale of friendship, love, and what lies hidden in between from *New York Times* bestselling author Lauren DeStefano.

www.laurendestefano.com
laurendestefano.tumblr.com
@LaurenDeStefano

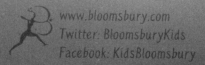

www.bloomsbury.com
Twitter: BloomsburyKids
Facebook: KidsBloomsbury